NO REGRETS

Visit us at www.boldstrokesbooks.com

By the Author

Emily's Art and Soul

Before Now

No Regrets

NO REGRETS

by

Joy Argento

2020

ISBN 13: 978-1-63555-751-0

This Trade Paperback Original Is Published By
Bold Strokes Books, Inc.
P.O. Box 249
Valley Falls, NY 12185

First Edition: November 2020

CREDITS
Editor: Cindy Cresap
Production Design: Susan Ramundo
Cover Design By Tammy Seidick
Cover Art By Joy Argento

Acknowledgments

Thank you to everyone who has encouraged me to keep writing, especially when I felt like throwing in the towel. Kate Klansky, Karin Cole, Jenny Argento, Toby Hewitt, and Susan Duffy, you are the people who kept me going. Georgia Beers, thank you so much for always answering my questions and for your generous advice.

Thank you to anyone that has taken the time to read my books, emailed me, or put up a review. I appreciate each and every one of you.

Beth

I sank down on the couch. All the air left my lungs and I struggled for breath. This couldn't be real. It wasn't real. It wasn't.

"Are you all right?" Jodi asked.

I nodded. Then shook my head. Then nodded again. Confused. No. I wasn't all right. My world had just come crashing down on me. I brought my eyes up to hers. Concern radiated out to me. To *me*. Her concern was for me. That made no sense. None of this made sense.

She sat by my side and I reached out to stroke her hair. Despite the news she had just shared with me, a tingle ran down my arm at the contact. I rested my forehead against hers. Tears leaked out of my closed eyes. "Oh my God," I whispered. It was all I could manage to say.

I felt her arms go around me and pull me in tighter. For a brief moment, the horrible truth left my mind and I was filled with the closeness of her. She felt so alive in my arms. How could she be dying?

I thought back to the first day I ever saw her, more than six years ago. She walked into my hair salon and plunked herself down in my chair. Her green eyes bright, her face lit up with a smile, she chatted away as I snipped new layers into her long brown hair. I found out later that she had just turned forty.

"Beth," she said, reading my name tag. "Pretty name. Short for anything? Elizabeth? Bethany?"

"Nope. Just Beth, plain and simple. That's me."

Her smile expanded. "I doubt that. Doesn't seem like there would be anything plain and simple about you."

I couldn't help but return her smile. She just had that effect on me. I assumed she had that effect on everyone.

"How long have you worked here?" she asked.

"Since I bought the place a year and a half ago." I had scrimped and saved every penny to make my desire to have my own salon a reality. Working for other people, especially the chain salons, had been a nightmare. This, on the other hand, was my dream.

"You own the place, huh? I'm impressed. I probably shouldn't admit this, but I usually cut my own hair. Been doing it for years. My daughter yells at me every time. She says I've had the same hairstyle since 1995. She wasn't even alive in 1995 so I'm not sure how she would know that. My name's Jodi by the way."

I mentally scolded myself for not asking. "Nice to meet you, Jodi. Your hair is pretty even. Looks like you've been doing a decent job—not that I'm suggesting you continue that practice." I tilted my head as I looked at her in the mirror.

"Can I get that in writing? To show to my daughter."

I laughed at her joke. "Sure. How many kids do you have?" I liked chatting with the clients. I truly enjoyed good conversation, and if they liked you they were more likely to return, which was just plain good for business.

"My partner and I have two. Well, I have two and she helps me raise them. My daughter's nine and my son's thirteen. How about you? Any kids?"

Partner? She didn't look gay. Not that I was a hundred percent sure what *gay* looked like. I didn't really know any gay women personally. If some of them looked like Jodi, then they might have slipped by my awareness. I didn't have anything against lesbians, although my church wasn't keen on the idea. I was a live and let live sort of person. Judging wasn't in my nature. I left that sort of thing up to God.

"Does that mean you don't have any kids or that you don't want to talk about it?" I realized I had been lost in my own thoughts and hadn't answered the question.

"One. She's seventeen."

I ran my fingers through her damp hair, pulling it out a bit at the ends to see if I had missed anything. I few stray strands were still longer than the rest.

"Wow. You must have had her when you were five because you certainly don't look old enough to have a kid that age."

I *was* young when I had her. I was the same age she was now. Her father, otherwise known as the *sperm donor*, to my family, left me as soon as I told him I was pregnant. I hadn't seen or heard from him since. I tried to get in touch once, shortly after Maddie was born, to tell him he had a daughter. I couldn't locate him, and I never tried again. Maddie asked me lots of questions about him when she was young but didn't seem to care anymore. She currently had more interest in running with the fast crowd and skipping school than discussing her parentage, and that included me. The less she knew about me, or heard from me, the better, in her opinion. I didn't let her get away with much and she didn't like it.

I brought my attention back to Jodi. "Thank you," was all I said, sure she wasn't interested in my life story.

The phone next to the cash register rang. Cindy, one of my three hair stylists, came out of the back room. "I've got it," she said.

"Hello. Shear Perfection. I'd be happy to assist you," she said, following the exact script my girls had to memorize. "Sure. Hold on please." She pressed the hold button and turned to me. "Beth, it's Robertson's Sign Shop. They want to know about stopping by to give you an estimate."

I thought for only a moment. I didn't like stopping when I was with a client. "Tell him I'll call him back after four."

Cindy finished the phone call and greeted a young woman who had just come into the shop.

I took a couple more snips on Jodi's hair and gave it a quick once-over with the blow dryer.

"You need a sign painted?" Jodi asked.

"Yes. The one out there isn't up to code. I didn't know it until last week when an inspector stopped by."

"I just happen to be a sign painter."

"You are not," I said, certain she was teasing me. "There, what do you think?" I fluffed up her hair a bit with my fingers.

"It looks great. Thank you." She brought her attention to me. "I really am a sign painter." She pulled a thin wallet out of her back pocket and fished out a business card. *Jodi Michaels—Sign Painter Extraordinaire*

"Extraordinaire?"

"It means I'm superb, exceptional, really, really good." Jodi laughed.

I smiled. "I know what it means. I've just never seen it on a business card before."

"Well, how are people gonna know how good you are if you don't tell them? My grandmother always told me it was okay to blow my own horn. Better to blow than to suck she always said."

"She did, huh?"

"Well, I might be paraphrasing, but it was something like that. I can give you an estimate for a new sign if you want." She put her hands up in front of her. "No pressure."

"I could use a sign painter extraordinaire, but I'm afraid you might be out of my budget. I don't have a lot to spend."

"I'm really good, I'm not really expensive, and we could probably trade part of it for haircuts for me and the kids, if you want."

I unhooked the plastic cape around Jodi's neck and shook it off behind the chair. It wouldn't hurt to get one more estimate. The first two were higher than I wanted to pay, and I had the one to schedule with Robertson's. "All right. Could we set up for a time to meet and I can tell you exactly what I need?"

"Absolutely," she said. "I'll bring pictures of my work and references." She stood and wiped a few stray pieces of hair off of her jawline. I wasn't sure how I had missed them.

"You have my number," she said.

"I do?"

"Yep. Right there on that little card I handed you."

I felt the blush of embarrassment creeping up my face as I looked at the card in my hand. "Of course." I waved the card in the air. "I have your number. I'll give you a call tonight if that's all right."

"That works. I'll be home."

"It's okay if I call you at home? Your partner won't mind?" I wondered how it was with two women together. I don't mean the sexual part. I could figure that out. I mean just the day-to-day stuff. Did one mind if another woman called the other? They must not, otherwise they wouldn't be allowed to be friends with other women. They would only be able to be friends with men. Who would want to be friends with men? Men were good for a lot of things like sex and fixing things. But for friends? I much preferred the friendship of women.

Jodi gave a little chuckle. "She doesn't care. I work out of my house. My workshop's in the basement. And that's my cell number."

We walked over to the cash register, and Jodi handed me her credit card. I ran it through and handed it back to the woman who would change my life in ways I couldn't even fathom in that moment.

Jodi

I walked out of that beauty salon with a little bit more of a spring in my step. The early June sun seemed brighter in the sky. I enjoyed chatting with Beth as she cut my hair. And my hair looked good. Besides making a business connection, I thought maybe I had made a new friend. I could use more friends. Claire and I had moved to Rochester with the kids over two years ago. Claire had made a few friends at work, but being self-employed and busy trying to establish my business had left little time to really get to know anyone. Now that business was starting to pick up, I thought it was time to add some new people to my life. I was friendly with some of the parents from the kids' school, but they were more like acquaintances.

Beth was the first person in quite a while to spark my interest. She was smart, easy to talk to, and very friendly. Of course, she might have been friendly because that was part of her business. Even if it was, she seemed genuinely nice. And she was very nice looking too. A little shorter than my five foot five with a slender frame that had curves in all the right places. I was happy in my relationship with Claire, but that didn't mean I couldn't admire the beauty of another female. Her blue eyes deep-set above high cheekbones looked even bluer against her tan skin. The short bob her honey-blond hair sported framed her face beautifully.

I found myself looking forward to her call. Most of the people I dealt with were men. It was nice when I came across a fellow female business owner.

I jumped into my Toyota and pointed it in the direction of home. I still had an hour and a half before Annie got home from school, and

Andrew had lacrosse practice so Claire was going to pick him up on her way home from work. I welcomed the quiet time to work on my website and get my newest designs uploaded.

I pulled into the driveway of our big colonial style house. It hadn't been my first choice, but Claire had fallen in love with it and I loved Claire and wanted her to be happy, so I agreed when she wanted to buy it. The one-car garage housed her Porsche when she was home which left me the parking spot on the side of our double-wide driveway. I could hear Tess barking before I even had my key in the door.

"Hey, girl," I called to her from the hallway. "I'll let you out in a minute." I threw my backpack on the kitchen table and headed to the laundry room. Tess, our Collie mix, could no longer contain her excitement, and her bark turned into a whine. I reached over the baby gate and scratched her head. "Okay, okay." I pulled up the bar on the gate to release it and set it to the side. Tess lurched forward but stopped short of jumping on me. Many months of training finally broke her of that behavior. Well, months and Claire bitching at me until Tess was trained. It was Claire's idea to keep Tess gated in the laundry room when no one was home. She would probably insist that we keep the kids there too if I let her. She'd never been a fan of kids or pets. In her opinion, kids were miniature adults who should be perfect at all times—just like she said she was as a child. To hear her tell it, she never did anything wrong. The only things we seemed to argue about was the kids and the dog. Oh yeah, and sex. Or lack thereof. But that was a whole other story.

I roughed up the fur on Tess's head and let her out the back door. She did her business in record time and came running back in. She followed me down to the basement and lay at my feet while I worked on my desktop computer updating my website.

I was still working when Annie got home from school.

"Hey, Mom," she called down the stairs to me.

"Be right up, honey." I saved my changes, shut down my computer, and nearly tripped over Tess as she raced up the stairs ahead of me, eager to greet Annie.

"Hey, baby." I leaned over to kiss Annie on the top of her head. She was growing like a weed and I knew I wouldn't be able to reach the top of her head much longer.

"I'm not a baby."

"You'll always be *my* baby." The younger of my children, I knew she would be the last. She favored me in looks, dark hair, green eyes, a quick smile, but had my mom's feisty personality and go-getter disposition. I had a much more laid-back personality, and while I went after what I wanted and had a good head for business, I didn't have the same drive that my daughter already showed at the tender age of nine.

I made her a quick snack, which she downed while she worked on her homework at the kitchen table. I pulled a package of chicken out of the fridge and got supper started. Claire liked to eat soon after she got home from work so she could relax in front of the TV for the evening.

The chicken was nearly cooked when I heard the door leading to the garage open. I turned in time to watch Andrew walk in followed closely by Claire.

"Hi, Andrew," I said. "How was lacrosse practice?"

"Okay," he answered. He was a boy of few words now that he was over the line that separated children from teenagers. He proceeded down the hall and up the stairs to his room.

"Hi, honey," I said to Claire.

"Hey, babe. Supper almost ready?" She set her briefcase on a kitchen chair. I knew it wouldn't stay there long. Claire was *an everything in its place* kind of person, and her place for her briefcase was upstairs on the desk in her office.

"About fifteen minutes," I answered.

"Great. I'm going to go up and change my clothes." She grabbed the briefcase and went up the stairs.

I wasn't sure why she needed to tell me that. She did the same exact thing every day after work, change from her work dress pants and button-down shirt into a T-shirt and jeans. She would run a brush through her short-cropped red hair and brush her teeth. Her routine never changed.

I turned my attention back to supper, putting the finishing touches on the salad.

"Annie," I said fifteen minutes later. "Please go let Claire and Andrew know that it's time to eat."

Annie walked to the bottom of the stairs and yelled, "It's time to eat."

"I could have done that," I told her.

"Then why didn't you?" She plopped down in her chair.

Claire walked into the kitchen just in time to hear her remark. "Watch your mouth," she told her.

Annie rolled her eyes. I watched the exchange without saying a word hoping it would end at that. Relief washed over me when Claire sat down without saying anything else.

Andrew joined us and I sat down with my family to enjoy our time together. Growing up, time around the table with my parents was a special time. A time to catch up on our day and share the important events of our lives. I wanted the same thing for my kids.

"How was your day, honey?" I asked Claire, trying to start the conversation.

She spooned mashed potatoes onto her plate. "Good. We had two new people start today so most of my day was spent showing them around." Claire worked for the Benderson Company. Their claim to fame was manufacturing components for computers and smartphones. She'd started with them eight years earlier in Denver. A promotion and a transfer to Rochester was what brought us here. I sold my sign making business there and attempted to reestablish it in this new location. I was doing all right, but it had been slow going. I glanced at the clock, wondering when Beth would call and hoping it wasn't during diner.

"Do you think they'll work out okay?"

"Seems so." She spent the next several minutes going into great detail about their credentials and her personal opinion of them. I listened and asked questions when she paused. When she finished her story, I moved on to the kids and asked them each in turn about their day. As usual, Annie was much more forthcoming than Andrew. Tess sat quietly under the table ever vigilant in case someone dropped a crumb she could scoop up.

I had just finished loading the dishwasher when my cell phone rang. "I think this is a business call," I called to Claire, who was already settled in front of the TV in the family room. "I'm going to take it downstairs."

"Yeah, okay," was her answer.

I pressed the answer button on my phone as I started down the basement steps to my work area. "Hello."

"Jodi?"

I recognized Beth's voice right away. "Yes."

"Hi, Jodi. This is Beth from the—"

"Hi, Beth." I interrupted her. "How ya doing?"

"Is this an okay time to call?"

I sat at my computer but didn't turn it on. I grabbed a legal pad and pen from a pile of stuff off to the side. Claire often complained that I didn't keep my work area clean enough and how could I be efficient that way, but I knew right where everything was. I know she was only trying to help me, but I liked things the way they were.

"Absolutely. I'm glad you called." And I was.

"Did you happen to notice the sign I have up at the shop now?"

I had noticed it, but only to read the name to see if I was at the right place. A neighbor had recommended it, but her directions to get there weren't the best. "Hmm, I didn't pay that much attention. I can swing by tomorrow to take a better look." I really should have taken a good look at it on my way out, but my thoughts had been more on the possibility of a new friendship. I hadn't admitted it to anyone, but I was lonely in this town, and while phone calls to my mom and friends back home helped, they didn't replace the day-to-day interactions.

"Oh, no need to do that. That's the sign I inherited when I bought the place. I want something that reflects my style a little better." She went on to tell me what the old sign looked like and what she wanted her new sign to be. She read me the dimensions she needed. We talked about material options and whether the sign would need to be lit at night. Once I had the important info down, I set the legal pad aside. We made plans for me to stop by the shop the following day at six when they closed. That would give me enough time to draw out some rough sketches and gather what I needed.

"How did your daughter like your haircut?" Beth asked, surprising me that she remembered.

I laughed. "She didn't notice."

"Kids," she said, laughing along. "How about your partner?"

"What about her?" Was she asking me about Claire?

"Did she notice your hair?"

No, she hadn't. I thought for a second how to answer that without making Claire sound indifferent. Claire noticed lots of things about me. My hair just wasn't usually one of them. "She didn't say anything about it. She'd had a really busy day at work. I think she was just distracted. But I love it in case you're keeping track."

"That's good. I would hate to think you didn't."

"I'll bet that doesn't happen too often."

"Every once in a while. I always hold my breath when I finish until they tell me what they think."

I smiled at this tidbit of information. Beth seemed like a very confident woman, sure of herself and her abilities. It was interesting to find out she had insecurities like the rest of us. But I knew exactly what she was talking about. I did the same things when I delivered a sign.

"How long have you been doing hair?" I asked, truly interested.

"Since I was about five and I cut my sister's. I thought it looked fabulous. My mother—not so much. I remember sitting in the *time-out chair* wondering what the heck I had done wrong."

"Sometimes mothers just don't understand."

"Are you speaking from experience?" Beth asked, her voice turning serious.

"Are you asking me about my relationship with my mother? Shouldn't I be stretched out on a couch with you sitting across the room, notepad in hand, Doctor?"

She missed the fact that I was joking. "I'm so sorry. I didn't mean to pry."

"I'm teasing. For the most part I have a really good relationship with my mom. When I was young, I thought she was perfect. As I got older, I realized she had her own dysfunctions. But I guess we all do. Well, everyone but me. I'm perfect. You probably picked up on that right away."

"I knew you had perfect hair. The rest I kind of just assumed."

I liked her. She played along.

Beth

I turned the open/closed sign around and moved out of the way to let Cindy pass by me. "Have a good night," I told her.

"You too. Don't work too hard."

"I'm just waiting for another sign estimate." I laughed. "Shouldn't be too much work at all."

"See you tomorrow," Cindy said and was gone.

Jodi showed up, portfolio in hand, moments later. She arrived, much like she did the first time she walked into the salon—with a huge smile on her face.

"Hey there," she said to me.

"Hi. Come on back to my office." I locked the front door. "Would you like some coffee? It's decaf. Or I can make tea."

"Coffee would be great." She followed me to the back. I poured two cups and handed her one. I put a small bowl of single serve creamers on the desk. I added two to my cup. Jodi took one.

"Do you take sugar?" I asked her. The packets were in the break room.

"Nope. Just cream."

"Me too."

I kept my desk pretty neat and organized but had moved the stacks of papers that I needed to go through to the top of the filing cabinet. The office was small, but minimal furniture made it user friendly. I pulled the more comfortable chair out from the desk and motioned for her to sit. I sat across from her.

"Ready?" She slid several sheets of paper out of her case.

"Hit me."

"Oooh, didn't know we were going there." She laughed.

"Shut up and show me…" I needed to choose my words carefully now, "your ideas for my sign."

"Sorry."

She didn't have to be sorry. I didn't mind the joke. I just didn't know how to respond. "You're fine. No need to apologize." I didn't want her to feel bad.

"I brought some photos of my work." She laid several pictures down across the desk. "Some of these are from Denver."

I leaned forward so I could see better. "Denver?"

"Yeah. I started my business there. Then started over again here."

"Wow. These are great." I picked up one that had the color combination that I wanted. I studied it closer. "You do very nice work."

"See," she said. "Extraordinaire."

"And quite modest too."

Her smile lit up the office. It was contagious. She showed me her sketches for my sign, and we went over pricing options. The cost was much lower than I expected, and I wondered if she was giving me a price break. In the end we decided on a figure that included a trade for ten haircuts for her and her kids.

"I'm so glad you came by, and I'm really looking forward to seeing the sign when it's finished. I'm sure you must be anxious to get home to your family," I said, hoping she could stay and chat a little longer.

She slipped her papers back into her portfolio and glanced at her watch. "I made dinner for them before I left, so they should be set for a while. What about you? Do you have a husband waiting for you at home? Where is your daughter tonight?"

"No husband," I admitted. "And my daughter has a sleepover with a friend." That gave me the whole evening to myself. Something I loved and at the same time hated. I hadn't had a *sleepover* myself in quite some time. That sad fact of life seemed to echo in my mind much more when I had alone time. While I was perfectly happy with my life—mostly—I missed having someone to cuddle up to at night and share my day with, and yes, I missed the sex. A lot. While I had become very proficient at the art of self-satisfaction it wasn't, well, very satisfying.

"Not even a hot date for you tonight?"

I laughed. "No. Not tonight."

"But it's Friday. Surely a woman as nice as you has the guys lined up around the block waiting to take you out."

I wasn't sure if she was messing with me or being sincere, so I just smiled.

"No guys lined up around the block?"

I shook my head.

"I really do find that hard to believe. Anyone special in your life?"

She was being sincere. I could not only tell by the way she asked the questions, I could *feel* it.

"No. Not right now. Not for a while." I somehow felt safe telling Jodi. She was just one of those people you knew you could somehow trust. "One of these days. I've been so busy trying to keep my daughter on the right track that I just haven't had the time. Not that I've had any offers lately."

"Must be tough raising a teenager on your own."

"At times it's wonderful. No one else to contradict my parenting style. And at times it's all I can do not to shoot her. No one ever tells you how hard parenting is. I think if we truly had a clue before we have kids then we wouldn't have them. The human race would have died out many moons ago."

"Wow. I like your honesty." She leaned forward as if sharing a secret. "I feel the same way, but all the parents I run into from the kids' school make it sound like their kids are their whole lives. Don't get me wrong, I love my kids and would kill for them. But you're right. It is so hard sometimes. And I know what you mean about not having someone contradict your parenting style. Claire and I don't always agree on the best way to raise the kids—or the dog for that matter," she added.

"That must be difficult."

"Sometimes it is. Claire is so great in a lot of other ways. I'm lucky to have her." She leaned back. "Is your daughter's father in the picture?"

"No. We were young." I shrugged. "He was foolish." My small laugh sounded more like a snort. I had gotten over it all a long time ago. It was Daniel who had missed out. Yeah, Maddie had missed out on a father. But Daniel missed out on being a father and getting to know her. He missed her first steps, her first words, her first time sitting on Santa's lap. I had been there for all of it and reveled in every minute. Of course, now he was missing the calls from school when she skipped classes and the back talk. So, I experience the good and the bad by myself. "I was a teenager when I had her. He didn't want any part of it."

"Wow. So young."

"We grew up together, Maddie and me. Sometimes I think we still are. I like to think I'm ahead of her on some things."

Jodi smiled. "Don't we all. You raised her all by yourself?"

I liked her. She was easy to talk to and seemed to really listen to me. Some of my friends seemed like they were just waiting for me to finish saying something so they could talk. Jodi wasn't like that as far as I could tell.

"My mom helped a lot. We lived with her for years when Maddie was little. My dad died when I was twelve, so she had plenty of experience raising a couple of kids on her own."

"That must have been hard losing a parent at such a young age."

"We did all right, my mom, my sister, and I. Then when Maddie came along it was the four of us for a long time."

"You've never been married?"

"No. Came close once, when my daughter was ten." I told her about my brush with happiness that came crashing down when my fiancé decided he didn't want me anymore, a month before our wedding.

"What an ass. I'm so sorry he did that to you."

"Yeah. He was an ass. I just didn't see it until that moment. It kind of made me gun-shy. It took quite a while before I dated again." I rarely shared that story with anyone, let alone someone I barely knew. But somehow it seemed okay to share details of my life with Jodi.

Jodi

It took almost three weeks to get the sign done for Beth's salon. I propped it against the wall and took several steps back. Yep. It looked good. I was sure Beth would like it. Jack, the guy I hired to hang it, would pick it up on Saturday and hang it on Sunday so it wouldn't interfere with business hours. I usually left that part totally up to him but planned on being there to make sure it was perfect. I liked Beth. I wanted everything to be just right for her.

"Jodi?" Claire called down the stairs to me.

"Be right up."

I found Claire in the kitchen pouring coffee into her travel mug. She had several, but this was one that she had purchased on a business trip to California. It was her favorite, and everyone in the house knew the rule was *hands off.* No one dared to touch it. There were several things in the house that had that rule attached to them. But it was understandable. Claire was six years older than me and had spent the majority of her life living alone. It was an adjustment to have a live-in partner with two kids. In order to preserve her sanity, I think it was important for her to stake her claim to her territory.

She turned toward me, cup in hand, screwing on the top. "I wanted to give you a kiss good-bye before I go to work," she said.

I wrapped my arms around her and looked up into her eyes. That was the first thing that attracted me to her four years ago. Her eyes. Deep blue with a touch of gray in the middle and green around the edges. She kissed me once on the lips.

"Gotta go, babe," she said, pulling away. "I'll be home at the regular time."

I resisted the urge to grab her ass as she walked toward the door. "Bye, honey. Have a good day."

She gave a little wave and was gone.

"Bye," I said to no one.

I proceeded up the stairs to get the kids ready for school. Once they were safely on their way to the bus stop, I went back downstairs. I wanted to check Beth's sign one more time. I really wanted her to like it and was looking forward to seeing her when it was hung.

❖

I woke with the sun, way before I really needed to be up. I was anxious to meet up with Jack and watch him hang Beth's sign. I pulled the covers back gently so that I didn't wake Claire and climbed out of bed. She lay totally uncovered in her short sleeve pajama top and yoga pants. She liked to keep the air conditioner on during the summer months and I found the nights too cold to sleep uncovered. It was only the beginning of June, so I knew I had many more cool nights ahead of me. I took a quick shower, dressed, and headed downstairs to make coffee. I let Tess out and got the paper from the end of the driveway while I waited for it brew.

I liked the quiet of a Sunday morning. It somehow felt more peaceful than the other days of the week. As a kid I was forced to go to church with my parents, but as an adult I leaned much more toward the spiritual side than the organized religion side. The only time you found me in a church was for a wedding or funeral.

Everyone in the house was still asleep as I put my feet up in the recliner, drinking my coffee and reading the paper. I was just finishing my second cup when Annie came down the stairs, hair a mess, sleep still evident in her voice and eyes.

"Hi, baby," I said. I moved the paper off my lap and opened my arms.

She was getting a little too big to be doing it, and I knew she wouldn't be doing it too many more times, but she curled up on my lap and let me wrap my arms around her. I kissed the top of her head and felt the warmth of her in my embrace. My little girl was growing up. The thought made me both proud and a little sad.

When she grew restless, we made our way into the kitchen and ate cereal together. I knew memories were made of the small things in life, and I filed this one away in my mind.

"Want to go with me today?"

"Where?" She poured more Kix into her bowl.

I told her about the sign and Beth's salon. She thought about it for a minute. "If I don't go can I have Marcy come over to play?"

"You'll have to ask Claire when she gets up. If she says yes, then you guys need to play outside. It's supposed to be a really nice day."

"Deal."

"And no fighting with your brother today while I'm gone." Of all the things the kids did that got to me, fighting was the worst. It drove Claire even crazier than it drove me.

She scrunched up her face.

"Hey," I said.

"Okay, okay."

We finished breakfast, I loaded food into the Crock-Pot, and set it so supper would be ready with minimal work when I got home. I went upstairs, kissed a still sleeping Claire good-bye, and headed over to Beth's salon.

Jack was already there with his nephew when I arrived. He had his ladder propped against the building.

The sun felt warm on my skin, a direct contrast to the air-conditioned temperature in our house. I stayed far enough back to have a full view of them working without risking being hit by something should they drop it from the ladder.

They had it hung and were just securing everything when I heard a soft voice in my ear. It sent a shiver down my spine.

"That looks so good." It was Beth.

I turned to look at her. I grinned, which she readily returned. "Hey there. You like?"

"I do. You did a wonderful job."

We stood in silence for a few minutes watching the men complete their work. We simultaneously applauded when they finished.

Jack gathered up his tools and his nephew and loaded them into his truck. Beth thanked them both and he was on his way.

She gave me a hug. "I am really pleased with it. Thank you."

"My pleasure." I meant it. I had enjoyed designing and working on this project for her. "Have you had breakfast?"

"I went to the earliest church service this morning so I could get here in time. So, to answer your question, no."

"My treat if you want to go grab some."

She shook her head. I thought she was going to say no, and unexpectedly, my heart sank a bit.

"You are not buying me breakfast. You gave me a great price on the sign, and you did a wonderful job. The least I can do is buy *you* breakfast."

"Don't be silly. You don't have to do that."

She shook her head again. "Come on. Let's go eat. We can argue about the bill later." I thought for a minute she was going to link her arm in mine. When she didn't, I felt an unreasonable pang of disappointment and laughed at myself for my foolishness.

Beth

I'd almost linked my arm in Jodi's but caught myself just in time. It was something I used to do with a few of my close friends, but I had never done it with someone I barely knew. I didn't think she noticed.

"Where were you thinking of going? There's a great little place a couple of blocks from here if you feel like walking, or we can drive if you would rather go someplace else."

"Walking works. Lead the way."

We walked side by side making idle chitchat until we came to Bangle Bagels Plus. Jodi held open the door for me. I blinked a few times to help my eyes adjust to the dim lighting compared to the bright sun outside. The smell of bacon and coffee wafted to my nose.

We were greeted by Lena. She had worked there as long as I could remember. I guessed her to be her mid-forties, but she was the type of woman that could have easily been ten years older or ten years younger. "Hi, Beth. How are you today? We don't usually see you here on a Sunday."

"I had a new sign for the salon put up today, by a sign maker extraordinaire." I winked at Jodi.

"I'll have to check it out," Lena said. She led us to a booth and poured two cups of coffee from the pot she'd been carrying.

She came back a few minutes later to take our orders.

"So, what made you move from Denver to Rochester of all places?" I asked Jodi. "Not that there's anything wrong with Rochester."

"Claire." She stirred cream into her coffee. "She transferred here for work. I grew up just outside of Denver and love it there, but you've got to go where the one you love goes. Just like Ruth from the Bible."

"Oh, you know your Bible, huh?" I asked, both surprised that Jodi, a lesbian, knew it and how shallow I was being thinking she wouldn't.

"I know the gay parts." She winked, teasing me.

I was pretty sure Ruth didn't follow Naomi for the same reason Jodi had followed Claire.

I felt the need to apologize. "I'm sor—"

Jodi put up her hands. "I'm joking. No worries."

A slight change of subject might be good, I thought. "What did the kids think of moving here? It must have been quite an adjustment for them."

"Annie was thrilled at the idea of a new adventure. Andrew, not so much. He didn't want to leave his friends or his father."

"His father?" I had just assumed Jodi and Claire used artificial insemination from a sperm bank, like I saw in a movie once. Maybe I needed to stop making assumptions.

"I was married. He wasn't a bad guy. Just not the right person for me. The penis thing kind of got in the way."

I opened my mouth to speak but laughed instead.

She joined in. "I knew I was gay since I was about fourteen. I just didn't realize it."

"Okay, now that one you're going to need to explain."

"I started having crushes on girls when I was in middle school. Mary Tanborn." She shook her head and smiled at the memory. "She was a year ahead of me in school and so beautiful."

"Did she know you liked her?" I sipped my coffee, realized it was still too hot, and added another container of creamer.

"Hell no. I didn't even let myself know how much I liked her. I justified my feelings, made up excuses of why I changed the way I walked from study hall to math class just so I could say hi to her in the hall. A part of me knew that I liked her way more than most girls like their friends. I also knew that the thought of being gay scared me to death. I shoved down any thoughts about being a lesbian. I didn't really let them surface until I was thirty-three. I had been married for almost eight years by then. I dated a few women after that and met Claire three years later. We've been together four years."

"Can I ask you a really personal question?" I hesitated, not sure if I should.

Jodi was quick to reassure me. "Of course."

"How could you be married to a guy and not know you were gay?" I really wanted to ask how she could have sex with a man if she was gay but thought that might be going too far.

But she seemed to read my mind. "You mean sleep with him?"

I nodded.

"Sleeping with him was okay. He was the one and only guy I'd ever been with. And at that point I hadn't slept with any women, so I had absolutely nothing to compare it to."

"And now?"

"It was nowhere near what I needed, and it didn't satisfy me. It took me long enough to figure out that I'm gay, but now that I did there's not a single doubt in my mind. It doesn't scare me anymore. If there was a magic pill that I could take that would suddenly make me straight, I wouldn't take it. I like who I am, and I like being with women."

I did some quick math in my head. "You were twenty-five when you got married?"

"Yeah. We had been going out for about three years. I was…" she raised her eyes to the ceiling, "twenty-two when I slept with him for the first time. We had been going out for a couple of months by then."

"That's late by today's standards."

Lena set a bottle of ketchup and a bottle of syrup on our table. "Food will be out in a few," she said and was gone again.

"Yeah. I think I slept with him more out of curiosity about sex than any real burning desire for *him*." Jodi continued when Lena was out of earshot. "I wanted to see what they got all worked up about in the movies and love songs."

"And?"

"And after I slept with him, I still didn't know."

"And with women? With Claire?" Jodi made it easy to ask questions. She didn't hesitate to answer them.

"Now I get it. It's so different for me. Of course, things aren't as hot and heavy with Claire now as they used to be. I guess that's natural when you've been together for as long as we have." There was a hint of sadness behind her words. I had the urge to put my hand on hers to comfort her.

"I was thirteen when I slept with my first boyfriend," I said, surprising myself at how much I was also willing to share.

"Wow. That's Andrew's age. I can't imagine that. But if any of the girls I liked had made any moves toward me my story might be much more like yours."

"It wasn't a really good decision on my part, that's for sure. I was nowhere near ready. I just wanted him to like me and thought that was a good way to do it."

"And how did that work out for you?"

"Like most relationships we have when we're kids. He left me for someone else. And the funny thing is that I heard she wouldn't sleep with him. Waiting for marriage and all that. He stayed with her all through high school. Just goes to show you what I sacrificed and how wrong I had been about it."

"Someone who really loves you will wait until you're ready."

"That is very true. I just didn't know it then. I don't think I even knew what love was then."

"And now?"

"Oh, I know what love is now. Just don't know if I'll ever find it."

"I have a feeling you will."

❖

I unlocked the front door of my house and went in. There was a pile of dirty dishes in the sink, and a glass lying on its side on the counter. A small puddle of milk had escaped from the glass and dried in a puddle. I shook my head. Maddie must have made herself breakfast. The kitchen, like the rest of the house, was small. Dishes in the sink made it seem even smaller.

"Don't have a cow, Mom." My daughter came into the room. "I'll clean the dishes as soon as I get back."

"Where are you going?" I wasn't crazy about how much makeup adorned her face, but mentioning it would only start an argument. At this stage of the game I had to choose my battles wisely. She had dyed her blond hair jet-black months ago against my objections. Too much makeup was just the latest phase in her attempt to establish her own identity. To some extent, I understood it. As her mother, I didn't like it.

"The mall to hang with friends. Linda's picking me up."

"When are you coming home?" I didn't want her coming home too late and having trouble getting up for school in the morning. She was slacking off her junior year of high school. My attempt to stress the importance of her grades for college landed on deaf ears. It was a fine line between being a good parent and being a nag. I knew nagging wouldn't work with her anyway.

"I don't know."

"I want you home by nine at the latest."

She let out a huff of air and shrugged.

"Do you hear me?"

"Yes."

I heard a car pull into the driveway. Maddie obviously heard it too. She grabbed her purse from the kitchen counter. "Bye," she said as she walked out the door.

I looked again at the dishes in the sink and rolled up my sleeves to wash them.

Jodi

"How was your morning?" Claire asked me, looking up from the Sunday paper. "You're getting back a little later than I expected."

"It was good. The client really liked the sign. We went out for a quick bite to eat afterward." I knew Claire wouldn't mind. She didn't have a jealous bone in her body, which I was both grateful for and didn't like at the same time. Not that I wanted her to limit my friends or who I spent time with, but it would have been nice to know, every once in a while, that she cared a little more than she seemed to. "Where are the kids?" I asked.

"Annie and her friend are in the backyard. Andrew is in his room, probably on his iPad."

She went back to reading the paper. It hadn't always been like this. When we first started living together after only three months of dating—I know, typical lesbians—she would greet me at the door with a huge kiss and a tight hug. It was one of the things I loved about her. I would find sweet little notes she'd left for me on the bathroom mirror or in my car, and she told me often how much she loved me. Her rule was that neither of us could leave the house without kissing the other good-bye. That was pretty much the only thing she still did. Well, that and occasionally telling me she loved me. I supposed it was normal for these things to slow down with time. In her mind she showed her love by going to work and paying the bills to keep a roof over our heads. I did appreciate her for that, but flowers once in a while would have been nice too.

I still tried to do sweet little things for her. I cooked her favorite meals, arranged a sitter so we could go out for date nights, and left little gifts under her pillow. She seemed to appreciate the gestures. I still loved her and truly believed she still loved me.

"I thought maybe we could go out to a movie tonight," Claire said, interrupting my thoughts. "I know you wanted to see that new Sandra Bullock one."

I smiled. Yes. She still loved me.

"That would be great. I'll call Roberta to see if her daughter can babysit." Roberta was our neighbor and her daughter Shelly was a typical teen always looking to make a little pocket money.

Shelly arrived right on time at 6:30. The dirty dishes from dinner were loaded in the dishwasher, and the kids were in the living room deciding what movie they wanted to watch on Netflix. I grabbed a light jacket because it was always a little too chilly for me in the theater, and Claire and I were on our way.

She drove, as usual. I think she liked the control it afforded her. I was fine with that. It gave me an opportunity to relax. With two kids underfoot and a business to run, I didn't get much down time.

"Popcorn?" Claire asked after buying our tickets.

I shook my head. The last thing I wanted was buttery fingers. I was hoping to be able to hold Claire's hand during the movie. We bypassed the snack counter and entered the dark theater. The previews were already in progress. Within minutes of sitting down, Claire reached for my hand. Yeah. She still loved me.

Beth

I glanced up at my new sign as I walked into my salon and smiled. Jodi had done a wonderful job. She had taken my vision and made it a reality.

"Morning, boss." Cindy greeted me with a smile. "Great new sign out there." She gestured with the pen she was holding.

"I know. Right? I'm very pleased." Cindy slid the appointment book toward me. I took a quick look. We had a pretty full day, good thing my other two hairdressers were coming in.

I put my lunch in the mini fridge in my office and came out just in time to see the first client arriving, an elderly woman with a bit of a shuffle in her step. She was accompanied by a man probably thirty years her junior.

"It's okay, Mom," he said to her. "I'm sure it will be fine."

"But they don't know what I like." She seemed distressed.

I glanced at the book before speaking. "Mrs. Ferguson?"

"Hi," the man said. He had piercing blue eyes and jet-black hair that had the slightest bit of gray starting at the temples. The cleft in his chin seemed to deepen with his smile. "Yes. My mom here is a little worried." He mouthed the word *dementia*. "Her regular hair salon closed and she's in need of a haircut and style."

"No need to worry, Mrs. Ferguson," I told her. "We can help you out with that."

She turned to her son. "Al, this isn't my place."

"I know, Mom. We talked about this. This is the new place."

"Are we gonna eat here?"

Al smiled at her. "No. This is where you are going to get your hair done. See, I brought the picture. He pulled a photo out of his shirt pocket and showed it to his mother before showing it to me. "This is how she usually wears her hair. I'm sure it would make her happy if you could do something close."

The picture was of his mother, obviously taken several years ago. There was a brightness in her eyes that was now lacking.

"Certainly. We can cut and style her hair this way." I looked from son to mother. "Mrs. Ferguson, we can do this for you here."

She nodded. "This isn't my usual place. I usually eat breakfast at Milton's Diner." I knew that diner had closed years ago.

Al shook his head. "This nice lady is going to cut your hair." He looked at me and tilted his head. "Maybe I should ask first." He smiled. "Are you the nice lady that will be cutting her hair?"

I smiled back. "Yes."

"Good. Okay, if I wait over there?" he said, pointing to the chairs lining the wall.

"Of course."

He handed me the photo and gently explained to his mother one more time what was going to happen. She followed me to the wash sink and sat down. She offered no resistance as I went about washing, cutting, and styling her hair, explaining exactly what I was doing each step of the way. Al sat quietly in the corner thumbing through an old copy of *People* magazine. All three styling chairs were full and a few more people sat in the waiting area by the time I was finished.

"Don't you look beautiful," Al said to his mother as I escorted her back to him. "Keep it," he said to me, handing me cash that included a very generous tip. "Thank you so much. You did a great job. Do you cut men's hair as well?" He glanced around the room, filled with women.

"We do indeed," I told him. Most of the men usually came in on their lunch hour or after work.

"Wonderful. I'll call and make an appointment. Who should I ask for?"

I looked down and realized I hadn't put on my name tag. "Beth."

"Very nice to meet you, Beth." He smiled wide, showing a row of perfect teeth. Braces no doubt when he was younger.

He took his mother's arm. "All set?"

"Am I here to get my hair cut or for breakfast?"

"You got your hair cut and it looks great. We can go out to breakfast if you would like." He gently guided her to the door. Looking back over his shoulder, he said, "Thanks, Beth. I'll call for that appointment."

I watched them go. His patience with her was remarkable. I wondered if it was a show for my benefit or if he was always that kind to her. My previous experience with men left me more than a little leery. Oh well, it didn't matter if he was all he seemed to be. It was none of my business.

I grabbed the sign-in sheet and called the next name on the list. Timber Larson stood up and headed in my direction. She was a regular and usually just came in for a trim. Her dark hair hung well below her shoulders. "Let's cut it short today," she said, to my surprise.

Cindy had just finished with a client when the phone rang, and she answered it. "Please hold," she said into the receiver. "Beth, it's Maddie's school."

Shit. What now. I looked at Timber.

"Go ahead," she said. "I'm not in a hurry." She sat in the styling chair that I pointed to.

"I'll take it in my office," I told Cindy.

I hurried back and took a deep breath before picking up the phone and hitting line one. "Hello? This is Beth Bellamy."

I listened intently as Mr. Sullivan, the vice principal, explained that there had been an incident involving Maddie and another student. Words were said, and a slapping match followed. Maddie was being suspended for a week. She would need to be picked up.

Son of a bitch. That was all I needed. There was no way I could leave the salon. I called my mother and explained the situation.

"Oh, honey, of course I'll go get her. Do you want me to drop her off at home?"

"So she can have the day off to do what she wants? No way. Can you keep her with you until I'm done here? I'll pick her up as soon as I can."

"Sure."

My mom. My hero. "Thanks. I really appreciate it. Put her to work, make her weed your garden or something."

My mom laughed. "I'll think of something. See you later."

I took several long moments to compose myself before going back out to my client. Cindy glanced over at me and I just shook my head.

"Everything okay?" Timber asked, catching my eye in the mirror.

I grabbed my spray bottle from the counter in front of her. "Just kid stuff. Nothing we can't get through." I forced a smile. "Um, maybe I should have asked you if you wanted a shampoo before I start spraying water on you." I held up the bottle. I needed to get my head back in the game here. My mom could handle Maddie till I picked her up. She behaved better for her anyway. There was no way I would let her disrespect her grandmother after everything she'd done for us.

"I washed it this morning," Timber said, bringing me out of my thoughts.

"I'm sor—" I started.

Timber turned her head toward me and held up her hand. She couldn't have been more than twenty-five, but she looked at me with knowing eyes. "It's no problem. Honest. Been through some stuff myself."

I nodded, appreciating her patience. "We're thinking about cutting this beautiful hair off, huh?" I lifted a few strands for emphasis.

"Is it long enough to donate what we cut?" she asked.

I said a silent prayer that Maddie would turn out as great as this young woman in my chair seemed to be. That kid was going to be the death of me.

❖

"Thanks, Mom," I said. Maddie hadn't looked me in the eye since I arrived to pick her up. "Did she give you any trouble?"

"Not at all. Good as gold." My mom was starting to show her age. I had offered, more than once, to dye her salt-and-pepper hair. She politely refused. "Come on, Mom," I'd teased her. "Don't you want to attract some hot guy?"

"Look who's talking?" she replied. "You should be the one looking for a guy. Don't you think it's time?"

"Time for what?"

"Time for you to live your life again. Maddie is growing up. She doesn't need your full attention anymore."

Today proved that she did indeed still need my full attention—and apparently more discipline.

"Let's go," I told Maddie. "Give your grandmother a hug good-bye."

Maddie did as she was told, followed me outside, and slipped into the passenger side of my car.

I had decided not to talk about this until the morning. I wanted to discuss it with a rational head and not from a place of anger. It would also give me the upper hand if I remained silent and let Maddie stew wondering when the hammer would come crashing down.

The ride home was completely silent, but my head was reeling. Everything I wanted—no—needed to say to her was running through my mind. All of the possible punishments I could bestow on her were on repeat.

"You'll be going to work with me in the morning," I told her when I pulled into the driveway.

I kept my face forward. I knew if I saw her roll her eyes at me I would lose it. What the hell was I going to do with her?

Jodi

Claire kissed me on the cheek. "See you later, babe."
I wiped my hands on the dish towel and turned for a hug. I wrapped my arms around her and pulled her in close.

"I'm going to be late." She wiggled out of my embrace and headed toward the garage door.

I snapped the dish towel at her, catching the corner of it on her butt. She gave me a dirty look.

I laughed. She didn't.

She didn't usually work on Saturdays, but every few months they had a teleconference with managers from the Colorado office. Claire could have joined in from her laptop at home, but she said it was more professional if she did it from her office at work. I suspected she was afraid of the kids making noise while she was on the call.

It was fine. I was taking Annie to get her hair cut at Beth's salon anyway. I was looking forward to seeing Beth again.

"Annie," I called up the stairs. "Are you ready to go? Come on, honey."

Andrew could have used a haircut too, but he balked at the idea and I didn't push it. He was responsible enough to spend a couple of hours alone while we were gone. He probably wouldn't come out of his room the whole time. Video games certainly kept his attention. I tried to limit it but was grateful at times like this that it would keep him occupied.

Annie trotted down the stairs and sashayed by me on her way to the door.

"Andrew," I called. "We'll be back in a little while. Remember the rules." Don't answer the door. Don't tell anyone who called the house phone that he was home alone, and no cooking or eating until I got back. And under no circumstances, short of a fire, was he to leave the house.

"Yeah, Mom."

I followed Annie out the door and locked it behind me. The drive was quick, and Annie and I chatted along the way. She was excited to try a new look with her hair. She had worn it long since she was about three and decided to get what looked like a modern day bob. She'd found a picture of a girl about her age on the internet with the exact haircut she wanted. She emailed me the picture so I would have it on my phone to show Beth.

"This is Annie," I told Beth when she greeted us from behind the counter. "Annie, this is Miss Beth. She will be the one cutting your hair."

"Nice to meet you, Annie," Beth said. "Your mom's told me a lot about you."

A slight blush traveled up to Annie's cheeks. Always shy around new people, she surprised me by looking Beth straight in the eye and responding, "Nice to meet you too." She reached across the counter to shake Beth's hand. I could see it wasn't just me who found Beth warm and welcoming.

"Maddie," Beth said to the young woman sweeping hair from the floor toward the back of the salon. "Come here. I want you to meet someone."

Maddie leaned the broom against the wall and headed in our direction. She forced a smile.

"Jodi, this is my daughter, Maddie. Maddie, this is Jodi and her daughter, Annie. Jodi is the one who did the new sign out front."

Maddie's smile seemed to turn genuine. "Oh yeah. Cool sign. I like it."

"Thanks." It was always good to get the stamp of approval. "Very nice to meet you. Do you help your mom out here on weekends?"

The corners of her mouth turned down. "Only when I'm being punished."

It was Beth's turn to blush. I wasn't sure if the red that colored her cheeks was from embarrassment or anger.

"Long story," Beth said, but offered no explanation. I probably wouldn't have either in a similar situation.

"Nice to meet you," Maddie said and went back to her broom.

"My mom has a picture of the haircut I want," Annie announced.

Annie nudged my ribs, my cue to pull out my phone and show Beth.

"Ah yes," Beth told her. "I think that will look very cute on you."

The blush on Annie's cheeks rose until her ears became involved in the embarrassment that a nine-year-old experienced for no particular reason.

"Do you need my phone as a reference?" I asked.

Beth smiled at me. "Nope. I've got this covered." I took a seat in the small waiting area and watched as my daughter was led to the same chair I had sat in weeks ago and the black plastic cape was draped over her shoulders. I couldn't hear their conversation but watched as they chatted away, and Beth snipped at her hair until it looked like the young girl's picture that Annie had found. I was impressed.

"What do you think?" Beth asked me when they were all done.

I nodded my approval. "Great job. Annie, do you like it?"

"I love it." She tossed her head side to side. She looked up at me and whispered rather loudly, "Ask her."

"Ask her what?" I whispered back, also too loudly, truly confused.

"Ask her if she wants to go to the play with you. I heard you and Claire talking yesterday. You said you wanted to go, and Claire said she didn't. She told you to see if one of your friends could go with you." Claire didn't seem to take much notice of the fact that I really hadn't made any true friends since moving here.

I glanced at Beth, who had obviously heard our less than quiet conversation. It really was a good suggestion. But I didn't want to put her on the spot in front of Annie. She probably wouldn't want to go to a play with someone she barely knew.

Several beats of silence followed as I tried to read the look in Beth's eyes. Annie tugged on my sleeve. I cleared my throat. "Well, the play is at Geva Theater a week from today at noon. It's called *Tom Hannagan Goes Home*. Have you heard of it?"

She hadn't. I continued. "Anyway, Annie's right, it would be great if you wanted to go. My treat. I already have the tickets." I was really hoping she would say yes, but fully prepared for her to turn it down.

"That would be great," she said to my surprise.

Annie smiled wide. Well, if I hadn't made a new friend, I knew that Annie had. Truth was, I was starting to consider Beth a friend. I was hoping she felt the same.

Beth

I followed the directions Jodi had given me and parked in front of the two-story house. I loved plays but hadn't been to one in quite a while. *Too much work and not enough play*, my daughter had often said to me. I realized she was right. This was the first Saturday I'd taken off since I opened the salon.

The house was bigger and nicer than I expected it to be. The sidewalk leading to the house was lined with the young flowers of June. I rang the bell and waited. The door was opened by a woman about my height, with very short, faded red hair and a thin face. My first thought was that a different hairstyle would suit her better, but quickly chastised myself for being judgy. Sitting by her side was what looked like a collie mix, tail wagging so hard that it made a thud as it thumped against the tiled floor. The woman gave me a smile and extended her hand.

"Hi," she said. "You must be Beth. I'm Claire."

I shook her hand. "Nice to meet you, Claire." I put the back of my hand out to the dog. "And who do we have here?" She gave my hand a sniff and then a quick lick.

"That's Tess. I'm sure she'll make a pest of herself," she answered. "Tess, go lie down."

"She's okay. She's beautiful." I ran my hand over the fur on her head.

"Come on in. Jodi will be down in a minute."

The large foyer was painted white, not eggshell, not off-white, not bone white, but pure white. I had never seen such a white white before. It extended up to the second floor. A chandelier hung from the high ceiling. An oak banister off to the left led up the stairs. Claire turned toward them and called up. "Babe, your friend's here."

Jodi came bouncing down. "Hi," she said to me. She had a big smile on her face. I had come to expect that whenever I saw her. I looked forward to it. I smiled back.

"Would you like a cup of coffee or something to drink?" Claire asked me.

"Sure, that would be great. Thanks." I followed her into the kitchen, with Jodi right behind me. It was as impressive as the foyer had been. The white cabinets stopped just short of the ceiling, and wicker baskets of varying shapes and sizes sat on top.

"Claire's collection," Jodi said when she noticed me looking.

"Very nice," I said more out of effort to be polite than any real admiration.

I could tell by Jodi's smile that she knew that.

Claire poured two cups of coffee and put them on the table. Jodi got a small container of half-and-half and put it on the table as well.

Claire sat at the head of the table and motioned for me to do the same. She pushed one of the cups in front of me.

Jodi handed me a spoon and sat across from me.

"Do you need sugar?" Claire asked me.

"Just cream," Jodi answered for me. I was surprised she remembered.

I snuck a look at Claire. I'm not sure what I expected, but this wasn't it. Jodi was very pretty. I guess I thought her partner would be equally nice looking. She wasn't. She wasn't what I would call ugly; maybe plain was the word that seemed to work best. She didn't seem as warm as Jodi was either, at least at first glance. I realized I was making assumptions again.

"Claire," I said. "Jodi tells me you work for Benderson. My uncle retired from there. How do you like it?"

She took a sip of her coffee before answering. "I like it a lot. I'm in charge of the warehouse. Inventory, that sort of thing. It's a busy place. I like to keep everybody hopping."

"That's great," I said. "Always good to like what you do for a living."

Jodi slid the container of half-and-half in my direction. "How was your morning?" she asked me.

"Fine. Maddie was in rare form this morning." I turned toward Claire. "Maddie's my daughter," I told her, not sure how much she knew. "She's seventeen."

Claire nodded.

"Anyway," I continued. "She usually argues with me about everything. But this morning she got up before I did and made me breakfast. I was kind of waiting for the shoe to drop. Wondering what she was up to."

"Did you find out?" Claire asked in a dull voice. *Dull.* That was the word I think I was searching for to describe her. Jodi seemed so animated, so full of life. Her partner, on the other hand, seemed dull, monotone. If Jodi was a movie she would be in full Technicolor. Claire would be in black and white. Grainy black and white. I wondered what Jodi saw in her. Maybe Claire was different when they were alone together.

I smiled, more at my thoughts about Claire, which I admitted to myself were not very charitable or Christian-like, than at Claire herself. "I have no idea. It kind of scares me."

"I can understand that. Teenagers in general scare me. Make me crazy in fact." There was no hint of a smile or that she was somehow kidding. I knew Andrew, Jodi's son, was a teenager. I wondered how hurtful Claire's statement was to her. I glanced at her but couldn't quite read her face.

I sipped my coffee and looked around the kitchen. It was remarkably clean for a house with children in it. No matter how much I picked up after Maddie, mine never even came close to this. "Where are the kids?" I asked Jodi. "I was hoping I would get a chance to meet Andrew and say hi to Annie."

"She had a play date and Andrew has lacrosse practice. I'm sure you'll get another chance."

"Thanks again for inviting me to this. I'm really looking forward to it."

Claire piped up. "You're doing me a favor. It got me out of going."

"Not a fan of plays?" I asked.

"Hate 'em. I find them so boring. Jodi's dragged me to enough of them. I'm glad she found someone else willing to go."

Yeah. I didn't like her. At all.

Jodi spoke before I had a chance to respond to Claire's comment. I wondered if she did it on purpose. "You're welcome. I'm so glad you agreed." She looked at her watch. "Maybe we should get going just in case it takes us a little while to park."

"Sure." A sense of relief washed over me at the thought of not trying to make further small talk with Claire.

Jodi got up, took my cup, and dumped it into the sink. She rinsed it, put it in the dishwasher, and rinsed the sink with the sprayer.

"Well, Claire," I said, pushing my chair from the table and standing up, "it was so nice meeting you."

"You too."

"Bye, honey." Jodi gave her a kiss on the mouth.

I turned my head, a little embarrassed at the intimate act and wondering if I would have turned away if Jodi was kissing a man good-bye instead of a woman. I wasn't sure.

As soon as we were in Jodi's car, she turned to me. "So, that was Claire."

I laughed. "I know."

"Sometimes she comes off a little…um…short. She doesn't mean it. She really is a great person."

"Of course she is. She must be, if you love her." And it was obvious that she did. I just wasn't sure why. "She was fine."

"Thanks." Jodi backed the car out of the driveway, deftly avoiding my car parked on the street, and pointed us in the direction of Monroe Avenue and the play I really was looking forward to seeing with her.

Jodi

I was actually glad it was Beth sitting next to me instead of Claire. It was funny, I didn't seem to miss Claire like I normally did when I was with Beth. Of course, I hadn't really spent too much time with Beth. During the play she whispered comments or funny remarks in my ear. Claire would never do that. Claire had a lot of great qualities. Her ability to enjoy a play was not one of them.

"I loved that," Beth said when the play was over. "I'm so glad you invited me."

"I'm so glad Annie insisted that I did."

She laughed. "She's a great kid."

"I like her." I folded my program in half and stuffed it into my back pocket as I stood up. "Would you like to go get some late lunch?" I pulled my phone out of my pocket, turned the ringer back on, and glanced at the time. "It's...wow, it's almost two o'clock already. Time flies when you're having fun. And, Beth, I did have fun. Thank you."

We shuffled down the narrow section between the seats to the aisle. "Won't Claire be expecting you back soon?"

I didn't have to pick Annie up until five, and Andrew got a ride from the Hendersons who lived next door and had a son in lacrosse as well. Claire would be fine without me for another couple of hours. "I have some time before I have to get home. But I don't want to keep you if you have other plans." I would have been disappointed if she said she did.

"Nope. Maddie is finally free and not shadowing me. I have to come up with a better punishment. That one is harder on me than it is on her."

"What's shadowing?" We worked our way through the thongs of people leaving the theater and headed in the direction of my car parked in the garage across the street.

"She got suspended from school last week for fighting."

"Ugh."

"Exactly. I wasn't going to let her make a vacation out of it, so I made her shadow me. When I went to work, she came with me and I gave her jobs to do. When I went to the store, she had to come with me. Everywhere I went she was my shadow."

"Oh yeah. I can see why that would be hard on you. How did she feel about it?"

"She hated it of course, but it wouldn't have been a punishment if she hadn't."

I found my car right away on the second level of the garage and pushed the button on the key fob to unlock the doors. It was always my job to keep track of where we parked whenever we went someplace because for some reason Claire had a hard time with that. But I didn't mind.

"Where is she today, now that she has her freedom back?"

"Believe it or not she opted to help my mom with gardening."

"Where would you like to go? Late lunch? Early drink? Middle of the day cup of coffee?"

Beth laughed. I liked the sound of it. "So many choices," she said. "Hmm." She tapped her finger against her lips that held a hint of red lipstick. "How about coffee? No. A drink. Are you hungry? We could do lunch."

"That's what I like. A woman that knows what she wants." I smiled wide at her, hoping she would get the joke.

She did of course. She slapped my arm playfully. "Hey."

"Hay is for horses."

"What are you, twelve?"

I shook my head. "A casualty of having a nine-year-old daughter. I need to stop quoting her." I backed out of the parking spot and pointed my car in the direction of the exit.

"I think it's adorable." I warmed to her bright smile. "If I quoted my daughter more often I would have to add a whole lot more swear words to my vocabulary."

"No shit?"

"No shit."

I tried to suppress a giggle, but it bubbled out anyway. It was refreshing having someone to talk to and especially someone who got my humor and played along. We chatted nonstop until I pulled into the parking lot of the restaurant that Beth suggested.

"Tell me more about you," Beth said once we were seated and had placed our orders. "How did you and Claire meet?"

I knew sometimes Claire didn't make a good first impression. She was the type of person you had to get to know before you warmed up to her. I wanted Beth to like her. It was important to me that my friends and partner got along.

"It was classic really. I saw her across a crowded room. It was love at first sight." I paused for effect. "The room was the emergency room. The crowd was made up of people waiting to be seen by a doctor. And the love at first sight statement I made up. It actually took about twenty sights before I fell for her. I really made her work for it."

Beth laughed. "Why were you in the emergency room?"

"Annie was spiking a fever. Claire was actually ahead of us in line to be seen but insisted we go first. She had sprained her wrist wrestling a bear trying to save a puppy." I smiled waiting for Beth's reaction.

"A bear?" She laughed again. "You're one hell of a storyteller."

"That's the story Claire likes to tell. That's what she told me and Annie that day. She had Annie in stitches, giggling her head off, as Claire described the bear in great detail. The truth is far less interesting. She tripped over a rock. I was so grateful she let us go ahead of her that I gave her my business card and told her if there was any way I could repay her to let me know. She called me the next day and asked me out."

"Wow. That's quite a story. So how did you make her work for it?"

"For quite a while, I told her I just wanted to be friends. She pulled out all the stops, flowers, romantic dinners, gifts. I think she fell for me before I fell for her. But when I did, I fell hard." Claire had been extremely sweet and attentive our first few years together. The business of our everyday lives had taken some of that away. But I knew deep down that sweetness was still there. It surfaced from time to time, and I was sure it would come back around in full force when life calmed down for the both of us. It the meantime it was nice to have a friend to do things with.

Beth

I had really enjoyed the play and even more so my time with Jodi. Her take on Claire was interesting. She certainly didn't present herself in the same light that Jodi portrayed her. Of course, I had barely met the woman. I decided to set aside my judgment of her and give her a fair chance. If Jodi and I were going to be friends, and it certainly looked like we were, then Claire was going to be in my life too.

My phone rang out a familiar ring tone as I pulled my car onto the expressway on my way to pick up Maddie. I pressed the answer button on my steering wheel connecting my phone to the car speaker. "Hey, sis."

"Where are you?" Jen asked without the need for formalities. "I went to get my hair cut and they said you weren't working today. Don't tell me you finally decided to get a life."

I shook my head, despite the fact that she couldn't see me. She was right. I didn't have much of a life lately. Well, more than lately. I hadn't had much of a life outside of work and my family in a couple of years. "As a matter of fact, I went to a play with a new friend today."

"I am so glad to hear that. Did you have fun?"

"I did. I'm on my way to Mom's to pick up Maddie. Want to meet me there and I'll order from Grubhub later for dinner?"

"Sounds like a plan. Roger is in Seattle again on business. See you in a bit." Her sister had hit gold when she met Roger. With her golden blond hair and bright blue eyes, she could have gotten just about any guy she wanted. Many had chased her. She let Roger catch her. They'd been married eight years, and if reality matched my perception, they had a rock-solid marriage.

Maddie was in the kitchen washing dirt from the garden off her hands when I let myself in the side door at my mom's. "Hey," she said with a slight sideways glance.

"Hi, honey. Where's Grandma?"

"Upstairs changing. You know how dirty she manages to get when she works in the garden. I don't know how she does it. It always looks like she rolled around in the mud."

I chuckled, both at the thought of my mom rolling in the garden and the fact that this was probably the most Maddie had cared to share with me in the past few weeks. I hoped this was the start of a new trend. But I knew how fickle teenagers could be at this age and set my expectations accordingly low. "How did it go today?" I asked, hoping to keep the conversation going.

"Good. We weeded everything including the front flower bed."

"I noticed how nice it looked when I pulled in."

"Maddie was a lot of help today," my mom said as she joined us in the kitchen. She still had a smudge of dried dirt on the side of her nose. I pulled a piece of paper towel off the roll, wet it, and wiped it off. "Thanks," she said. "Did I miss anywhere else?" She turned her head from side to side.

"Nope. That's it. I'm glad Maddie was a help today."

"Knock. Knock." My sister entered the kitchen, stopping to give Maddie a hug.

"This is a nice surprise," Mom said. "All my girls together."

"Beth invited me to dinner. Didn't she tell you?"

"I just got here myself. Didn't get a chance yet." I turned to my mom. "I invited Jen for dinner."

"I heard," she said with a laugh. "I'll have to see what I can whip up."

"No need," Jen said. "Beth is treating us to Grubhub. Right, Bethy?" I hated the nickname she'd given me as a kid. Of course, she usually added an insulting word to it, Messy Bethy—making it sound more like Methy Bethy. Or Deafy Bethy. She dropped the insult when we were teenagers. Thank God.

I'd asked her a few times not to call me that, but once in a while, it still slipped out. I chose to ignore it. "I did. I had a late lunch, but I thought I could order something in a little while."

"Can we get Chinese?" Maddie piped in.

We spent the next fifteen minutes discussing where we should order from and what each person wanted. Eighty-five dollars later, the meal was ordered, and we were seated around the kitchen table in the same spots we sat in when we were growing up. The table had been replaced since then. The scratches that Maddie put in it dragging her metal toy truck across it when she was three, or the dent left when Jen dropped a large rock she'd found for a school project, only a memory now. The rest of the kitchen was also shiny and new. The yellow flowered wallpaper replaced with a pale green paint and the old kitchen cabinets now sported new oak doors with brass knobs. The outward appearance of the kitchen had definitely changed, but the warmth and love that I felt sitting there with my family certainly hadn't.

"How was the play?" Mom asked.

"Really good. It was so nice to take a day off."

"And who's this new friend? With the schedule you've been keeping lately with your salon I'm surprised you had time to meet anyone."

"Actually, she's the one who made my new sign."

"I saw that today. It looks great. By the way, I still need my haircut." Jen shook her locks for emphasis. "But I interrupted you. Sorry. Tell us about your friend. What's her name?"

I smiled at the thought of Jodi. I truly did enjoy her company. I proceeded to tell them about her, leaving out the mention of Claire or the fact that she was gay. I'm not sure why. It wasn't that I thought she was lesser because she was a lesbian. Maybe I was afraid they would think less of her if I mentioned it. I silently scolded myself for the omission.

"So, she's married?" my mom asked, coming to that conclusion, I'm sure, because I mentioned Jodi's kids.

I had another opportunity to fill in the blanks and once again failed. "Divorced."

The sound of the doorbell stopped any further questions. Maddie got up to collect our food as my mom rose to get plates and silverware.

My mind went once again to Jodi. I had the feeling we would be good friends. At least I hoped we would.

JODI

"Hi, Mom," I said, hitting the speaker button and setting my phone on the counter as I loaded the last of the breakfast dishes into the dishwasher. "How are you?" Of all the people I missed in Denver, I missed my mother the most. Our regular once a week lunch had been replaced by a once a week phone call.

"I'm doing well, honey. How are you? How are the kids? Claire?" She liked to cram all of her questions in at once. I smiled at the familiar exchange. I filled her in on everyone, told her about the latest happenings with my business, and asked her about my dad. She got me up to date on all the hottest news in Denver.

Claire came up behind me just as I hung up the phone. To my surprise, she wrapped her arms around me and said in a low voice, "What's on the agenda for today?" She hadn't initiated any kind of physical contact in quite a while. Even a hug was hard to come by these days. She had a rare day off and the kids were still at school.

I turned in her arms to face her. "What would you like to be on the agenda?" I responded in the most seductive voice I could muster. My lips were inches from hers. I wanted to kiss her but held back. I wanted her to take that step toward me. I held my breath. Hoping.

She let me go and took a step around me, grabbing a piece of bacon from the plate I hadn't put in the refrigerator yet. "I was hoping you would go to the antique store in Canandaigua with me." She stuffed the bacon in her mouth.

"Oh. I was hoping you had something else in mind."

"Like what?"

I shook my head. "Nothing."

"So?"

I wiped my hands on the dish towel. "What?"

"Want to go to look at antiques with me?"

At least she was asking me to be with her. That meant something. Didn't it? "Sure. Are you looking for anything in particular?"

"I thought it would be nice to get a small table for the entranceway."

I thought for a few moments. Andrew had lacrosse practice and didn't need to get picked up till five thirty. Annie would be getting off the bus at three. We had plenty of time. I still felt a pang of disappointed and reprimanded myself for it. Of course, sex slowed down when you'd been together as long as Claire and I had been. At least that's what Claire told me. And I had no reason to doubt her. But doubts did creep in. I pushed them aside. Claire showed her love for me and the kids in so many other ways. We had a roof over our heads and food on the table. I didn't want for much. My *love language* was physical touch, and I knew Claire's was gifts. I had read that book and answered all the questions—for the both of us. Claire had no interest in reading it. So when Claire bought me a new book or kitchen gadget, I knew she was showing her love for me. "A table might be nice there."

"I thought so. And we can look for another light for your work area downstairs. You mentioned the other day that yours was flickering."

There she was again—showing me love in the way she knew how. I could let the other stuff go. "Let me just start the dishwasher and I'll be ready."

She gave me another quick hug—two in one day. Maybe things were looking up. "I'll meet you in the car. You can drive. A table would fit better in your car anyway."

I popped a detergent pod in the dishwasher, closed the door, and pressed start. My cell rang before I had a chance to walk out of the house. A quick glance at it told me it was Beth. I was torn between getting out to Claire and making her wait while I talked on the phone. I compromised. "Hey, Beth. I'm just about to head out with Claire. Can I call you back?"

"Of course. I hope you have a good time."

"Thanks. Will you be around later today?"

"Yep."

"Okay, talk to you later."

I pressed the end button and stared at my phone for a long moment. I called Tess, put her in the laundry room, and headed out to Claire, my mind still on the phone call from Beth. And hoping it wouldn't be too long before I could call her back.

Beth

I slipped my cell phone back in my desk drawer, surprised by my disappointment. I was looking forward to talking to Jodi more than I had realized. Well, my question for her would just have to wait. It was a slow day at the salon. Luckily, we had enough hopping days to make up for days like this. I opened my computer and clicked on my accounting software. I took advantage of the lull in business to enter my latest receipts, something I often put off in favor of cutting and styling hair. It was actually the interactions with the clients that I liked best. My girls could handle the few clients that were on the schedule, and if we got busy because of walk-ins, I was nearby to lend a hand.

I was still in my office a few hours later when my phone rang. I jumped at the sound, engrossed in my work. I picked it up and pressed the answer button without looking at the caller's name. "Hello."

"Beth?"

I couldn't help but smile at the sound of Jodi's voice. "Hi there."

"Sorry it took so long to get back to you."

"No problem. Did you have a nice time?" I closed my laptop and leaned back in my chair.

"It was okay."

"That doesn't sound too thrilling."

"We went antique shopping. More Claire's thing than mine. But it was fine."

Cindy took that moment to pop her head in my office. "Mrs. Ferguson and her son are here. He asked for you. Can you come out or should I have Rachel help them out?" I put my hand over the mouthpiece on my phone. "No. I'll be out in a minute."

She nodded and backed out of my office, quietly closing the door as she did.

Jodi obviously heard her—or me. "Do you have to go?"

"In a minute. I wanted to know if you would like to come over for lunch tomorrow. Maddie will be at school—at least she better be. I have to be there in the morning because I have a repair guy coming over to look at my dryer. I thought maybe I'd stick around and make you lunch. If you're interested."

"I would love to."

I relaxed. She said yes. "That's great. Listen, I do have to go. I'll text you the address. Does noon work for you?"

"Absolutely."

We said our good-byes and I went out to the shop and up to the counter where my client was waiting. "Hello, Mrs. Ferguson," I said to the elderly lady. "Mr. Ferguson." I nodded at her son.

"Al. Please."

"Al," I repeated. I turned to his mother again. "How are you today?"

"Was I here before?" she asked.

Al had his arm around his mother's shoulder. "This is where you get your hair done now. You were here a few weeks ago. You were very happy." He addressed me. "She really was. She may forget why she's here, but once home she admired herself in the mirror and commented on how nice her hair looked."

"I did?" she asked him.

"You did." He smiled at her. His smile turned to me. "We were both very pleased with your services. I'm sorry to drop in without an appointment. I hope it's okay."

"Of course. It's no problem. Walk-ins are always welcome."

Mrs. Ferguson looked at her son and smiled. "Walk-ins are always welcome."

"That's good news, Mom."

"Oh yes. I can get my hair done." Her moment of clarity surprised me. Al winked at me. He was obviously used to it.

"Same style as before. Do you need to see the photo again?"

I prided myself on remembering clients and their preferences. I shook my head. "I've got this. Are you ready, Mrs. Ferguson?"

"For what?"

Al gave a little smirk and shook his head. "For your hair trim and style."

"Yes. Of course. That's why we're here isn't it, silly?"

I led her back to the wash sink and helped her into the chair. She leaned her head back like an old pro and I went to work.

"Another great job," Al said when I returned his mother to him. "Shall we set up another appointment in about a month?" He handed me several folded bills to cover the appointment and a hefty tip.

I handed him a card with the new appointment, and they took their leave. The only other client in the shop was in Cindy's station and they chatted away as she snipped her hair. Rachel was sweeping the floor. I held out my hand for the broom and she passed it over, a cloud of confusion on her face. "You can go home. I'll pay you for the whole day. No need to hang around. I'll finish this."

"Wow. Thanks." She grabbed her purse from the backroom and was gone before I had a chance to change my mind.

I finished sweeping the stray hair from the floor and deposited it in the tall trash can that sat just out of the clients' view. My mind went to Jodi and lunch. I liked to cook, but cooking for just Maddie and me often got boring. And Maddie didn't seem to appreciate it when I whipped up something special. I wasn't sure what I was going to make. I should have asked Jodi if she had any special likes or dislikes. I tried to remember what she had eaten the couple of times we had gone out together. She wasn't a vegetarian…and she didn't seem to be staying away from gluten—which was all the rage these days.

I wondered if I should go simple, with just sandwiches and chips. Or fancy, with my world famous lasagna. Okay, it wasn't world famous. But my family seemed to like it. I would stop at the store after work and get all the fixings. I could put it together while the repairman worked on the dryer. I was so deep in thought that I didn't even notice that Al had come back in. I turned with a start at the sound of my name.

Al looked like he tried to suppress a laugh. "I'm so sorry. I didn't mean to startle you. I think my mother may have left her…oh, there it is. Her handkerchief." He pointed to the shampooing chair. I hadn't even noticed it there. "She usually keeps it in her pocket. For some reason fidgeting with it helps her stay calm."

"Of course." I retrieved it and handed it to him.

"I also what to thank you for being so good with her. I never know how people are going to react. Sometimes they get flustered when she goes off the rails with the dementia." He seemed genuine in his gratitude.

"It's no problem. I understand."

"Well." He held up the handkerchief. "I better get this back to her. She's like a kid without her favorite blanky."

I nodded. He headed for the door, turned at the last second, waved, and was gone. What a nice man, I thought. He really does care for his mother.

"Cindy, I'm going back to my office. Let me know if you need me."

"Will do, boss," she said and turned her attention back to the woman in her chair.

I sat in my chair and pulled my phone from my desk. I opened my notes and started my shopping list. I was determined to cook Jodi the best lasagna she'd ever eaten.

I looked at the clock one more time. The repairman was just finishing up and I hoped he would be on his way before Jodi arrived. I still had half an hour before she was expected.

"All set, Ms. Bellamy," Joe, the repairman, said. "I'll just leave this here for you." He set the bill on the kitchen counter and pushed his black rimmed glasses farther up his nose. "You've got yourself a new thermal fuse. It's good to go."

"Thanks, Joe." I walked him to the door.

"Let me know if you have any other problems."

I nodded, thanked him again, and walked back to the kitchen. I took the meatballs from the oven and added them to the pot of homemade sauce on the stove. I put the lasagna where the meatballs had been. If I had planned this right and Jodi was on time, we would be sitting down to eat about forty-five minutes after she arrived. I set the table in the dining room. The kitchen was too small for a table, and Maddie often used the dining room table as a catchall. It was a bone of contention between us. I made sure that she had cleaned it off before going to bed the night before.

I didn't know why I was restless—almost nervous. I hadn't entertained anyone but my family in my home in quite a while. My sister was right. I really did need to get a life. Maybe this was the first step in the right direction. I was very grateful for the possibility of a close friend. There was just something about Jodi that I really liked. She was easy to talk to and so easy to laugh with. I needed that.

I did one more quick tour of the house to make sure everything was neat and clean. Keeping up with that with a teenager in the house was often a challenge. Satisfied that everything was in order, I went upstairs and inspected myself in the full-length mirror in my room. I ran a quick brush through my hair and brushed my teeth. What the hell was wrong with me. This was a friend. It wasn't a date. It wasn't the pope. It wasn't—I didn't know what. It was a friend.

The doorbell rang when I was halfway down the stairs. I rushed the rest of the way, stopped just short of the door, and took a deep breath. I smoothed down the front of my pants and pulled my shirt down in the back. Stop it, I thought. Just answer the damn door.

"Hey there," I said as I opened the door.

"Wow. It smells so good in here." Jen pushed past me. It wasn't Jodi. I tried to hide my disappointment and surprise.

"What are you doing here?"

"That's a nice welcome." She turned and hugged me. "I went by the salon again. Still trying to get a haircut. Couldn't believe I missed you again. But Cindy said you were home today, so I thought I'd stop by. What are you cooking? Am I in time for lunch?"

My mind raced trying to figure out a way to get her out without hurting her feelings. I wasn't sure why I didn't want her to stay and have lunch with us. Actually, I did know. I didn't want to share Jodi. At least not this early in getting to know her.

My sister made her way to the kitchen. She picked up the lid on the saucepan, peeked in, and took a whiff. She tilted her head as she looked at me. "Are you expecting company?" She caught sight of the dining room table set for two, and her face lit up. "Do you have a date?"

"I do," I said. "But it's not what you think. It's Jodi. My friend I mentioned that made my new sign."

Her face dropped. "Damn. I was hoping it was a man. Oh well." She put the lid back on the pot. "What time is she supposed to be here?"

I looked at the clock on the stove. "In about ten minutes."

"Okay if I stick around and meet her? I'll get out of your hair after that."

I mentally kicked myself for the relief I felt. I was being ridiculous and I knew it.

"Of course. Want something to drink?"

"Sure. A margarita would be nice."

"Ha ha. It's not even noon. I was thinking more like a glass of juice or a cup of coffee."

"Geez. I was kidding. A cup of coffee would be good if it's already made. Otherwise I'll settle for juice."

"Juice it is then." I opened the fridge door and peered in. "Apple or grape?"

Jen grabbed a glass from the cupboard. "Apple."

I handed her the bottle and she poured herself some. She followed me into the living room and sat across from me. We made small talk for about twenty-five minutes. I noticed her check her watch several times, bringing home the fact that Jodi was late. I excused myself to take the food out of the oven and returned to the living room.

I was relieved when the doorbell finally rang.

"I'm so sorry," Jodi said when I opened the door. "Claire called just as I was about to leave, and I had trouble getting her off the phone. When she has time, she calls me on her lunch hour. Oh hi," she said, noticing my sister sitting on the couch. She extended her hand. "I'm Jodi. I'm guessing your Beth's sister." She looked from Jen to me. "You two look so much alike."

My sister stood up. "Yes. I'm Jen." She shook the hand Jodi offered. "Nice to meet you. I was just about to go."

"You aren't staying for lunch?" Jodi asked her.

"Not this time. I have some errands to run. But I'm glad we had a chance to say hello." She gave me a hug, said her good-byes, and left.

"Your sister and you have the same sparkle in your eyes," Jodi said. "Both beautiful."

I felt a heated blush rise up my neck to my cheeks. "Thanks," I said, not quite sure why I couldn't meet Jodi's eyes. "Lunch is ready. I hope you're hungry."

"What can I do to help?"

"You can tell me what you would like to drink." I ran through the list of possibilities. She chose the merlot. I handed her the bottle and my fancy battery operated corkscrew. I watched her open it like she was an expert.

"What else can I do?"

"Nothing. Everything is done. Go ahead and sit down." I waved in the direction of the dining room. We would still be close enough to chat as I got the food ready.

"You shouldn't have gone to all this trouble," Jodi said. I set the pan of lasagna next to the bowl of meatballs and returned to the kitchen for the garlic bread.

"No trouble at all. I enjoyed it." I sat across from her and said a silent prayer, thanking God for the blessing of this food and my new friend.

Several seconds of silence followed as we filled our plates.

"This looks so good. I'm not used to having someone else cook for me." Jodi took a large bite of garlic bread.

"Claire doesn't cook?"

Jodi shook her head. "She knows how to make eggs and she makes the stuffing for Thanksgiving. I'm not sure she knows how to make anything else."

"That's sad. So, she would starve if you didn't cook for her?"

"Not at all. She knows all the best restaurants and she's not afraid to use them."

I laughed.

"She also has Mark's Pizza on speed dial."

Time for a change of subject. I wanted to know more about Jodi. I really didn't care about Claire. "What's it been like for you to move here? Do you miss Denver?"

"I would never say this to Claire…"

Claire again.

"…but it's been damn hard. I miss my mom and my friends."

Despite my reservations, I needed to ask. "Why wouldn't you tell that to Claire?"

Jodi hesitated and I wondered if she didn't want to tell me. She must have read my mind—or my face—because she said, "I'm just trying to figure out the best way to say this." After several long moments, she continued. "I want Claire to be happy."

"Of course." I could only imagine that Jodi would sacrifice her own happiness to assure Claire's.

"She was so excited when she got the promotion and the opportunity to move. Claire's originally from Chicago and has no real attachment to Denver. So, for her it was no big deal to pick up and leave. For me and the kids it was a different story. We've never lived anywhere else. Our roots are there."

I nodded. I couldn't imagine picking up and leaving Rochester and my family.

Jodi continued. "It was especially hard for Andrew. Annie seems to be able to adapt to anything. Not to mention the struggle to reestablish my business here. I just don't want Claire to know how hard it's been."

I appreciated her honesty and my heart hurt for her.

"Don't get me wrong. Claire has been great. She pays the majority of the bills. She is very generous with her money. I've never had to worry about where our next meal was coming from."

I imagined that Claire liked the control that afforded her.

"I kept in touch with my friends for a while after we moved, but the distance seems to have made a difference, and one by one, we sort of lost touch. It's been quite lonely to say the least."

For a second I thought she was going to cry, but she looked me straight in the eye and continued. "That is why I am so thankful to have met you. You are like a ray of sunshine in my cloudy life." She smiled.

I felt the sincerity in her smile and returned it. "I feel the same. My life has been so wrapped up in my daughter and business that I've let friends slip away. I truly enjoy your company."

She held up her glass of wine. "To new friends and fresh starts."

I clinked my glass to hers. "Amen."

"Did you get your dryer fixed?" she asked. The fact that she was changing the subject didn't escape my notice.

"I did. It's been broken for a week. I never thought I would be grateful to do laundry."

She laughed. "And work? Will you be going to the salon later or are you taking the whole day off?"

"Hmm, that's a good question. I don't know. I have plenty I can catch up on around here. On the other hand, it feels very weird to take a whole day, other than Sunday, off."

"Ah, the joys of owning your own business. I understand. I hired a woman to help me with mine but had to fire her for stealing my computer. I should have known it wouldn't work out. She was fresh out of prison."

I stopped with a fork full of food halfway to my mouth. "Seriously?" She snickered. "No. Not seriously."

I couldn't help but laugh. "You're quite the smart-ass, aren't you?"

"Well, most people just call me an ass. Thanks for also saying I'm smart." She took a large sip of her wine.

"You're welcome." I shook my head. "But I doubt anyone would call you an ass. I can think of a lot of words to describe you. Ass wouldn't be anywhere on the list."

"I can think of a lot of words to describe you too."

She had me intrigued. "What words would you use?" I was quite aware of the fact that I was asking for a compliment.

Luckily, she obliged. "Friendly, funny, beautiful—inside and out. And that's just off the top of my head. I could dig in and add a couple dozen more."

"You left out intelligent."

"I said I wasn't done. Intelligent, modest, short."

"Hey!"

"Let me finish. Short on days off."

"Nice save." I smiled. Jodi was so great to be around. I poured us each another glass of wine. What a great afternoon. The visit wasn't even over and I was already looking forward to the next time I could see her.

Jodi

I had thoroughly enjoyed my afternoon with Beth. The great food was topped only by the great company. It had taken some time, but I finally found something to be excited about in Rochester. I thought I might even be developing a little crush on her, which didn't mean I didn't love Claire. I did. Crushes were a perfectly natural thing, even when you were in a loving, committed relationship. I could have a crush and still keep things in the friendship mode. Of course, I wouldn't be sharing that bit of information with Beth. Straight women tended to act weird and often backed away when confronted with such truths.

I got home several minutes before Annie got off the bus. I knew I was cutting it close but was just so reluctant to leave Beth's. Annie knew the combination on the garage door, so she could have let herself in, and nine was certainly old enough to be by herself for a little while, but I liked to be there when she arrived.

I took care of Tess and was just letting her back in when Annie burst through the front door. Tess greeted her with a tongue bath.

"Only one more week of school," she announced to Tess and me. "And my teacher said we don't have to do any more homework."

"Yay," I exclaimed. "Now you have plenty of time to help with more chores around the house."

"Boo."

"I'm just teasin' ya. Run upstairs and put your backpack in your room and I'll make you a snack."

Annie did as she was told and returned in record time. I set a half of a peanut butter and jelly sandwich in front of her and sat on the other side of the table. The end of school meant the end of fourth grade for Annie and seventh for Andrew. It also meant the kids would be going to Denver soon to spend time with their father. I wanted to fill myself with their presence until then.

Annie and I chatted while she ate, and then she helped me make a salad for dinner. We ate as soon as Claire got home so we could go to Andrew's last lacrosse game of the season.

"He's not doing too great, is he?" Claire whispered in my ear later.

I shook my head. Andrew loved the sport, but it wasn't his strong suit. But I had to give him credit for giving it his all. I wished Claire would give him a little more credit too.

Annie tugged on my sleeve. "My butt's falling asleep."

I laughed. But I knew what she meant. The hard bleachers where definitely hard on the derriere. "Come here, baby. You can sit on my lap."

"I'm not a baby," she said as she climbed up.

"Aren't you a little too big for that?" Claire asked her.

I felt myself tense. Annie ignored the question and Claire didn't push it. I allowed myself to relax and enjoyed the rest of the game.

"We lost," Andrew said after the game.

"You almost won," Annie informed him. "It was close."

I ruffled the hair on his head. "You did great."

"Mom," he exclaimed and did his best to put the strands back in their proper place.

A quick stop at Burger King to get dinner for Andrew and a snack for Annie and we were on our way home. My phone pinged with a text as we pulled into the driveway. I waited until we were in the house to pull it from my pocket to take a look.

It was from Beth. I smiled.

Beth

I watched a glowing ember float up from the fire pit and disappear in the cooling night air. I sipped my beer and swiped at a drip running down the neck of the bottle as Claire droned on about work and her place in its hierarchy. I had invited Jodi, Claire, and the kids for an evening in front of the fire pit, drinks, and s'mores. I thought it was a good way to get to know Claire, give her a fair shake, maybe see what Jodi saw in her.

Jodi poked a marshmallow on one of the sticks I had purchased for the evening and held it over the fire pit, turning it deftly so it browned to perfection without burning and handed it to Annie.

"Wow. I'm impressed," I told her.

She turned with a smile on her face. "One of my many talents."

"Marshmallow roaster extraordinaire."

Claire leaned forward and gave Jodi's knee a squeeze. "She is a woman of many talents. She's also great at starting fires."

"Like an arsonist?" I joked.

Jodi laughed. "No. Like in fireplaces or"—she waved her hand toward the fire—"fire pits. The secret is this little starter log. They catch quickly and spread fast."

"Oh, you're too modest, babe," Claire said. "I have a hell of time, even with those little sticks. Jodi's great at it."

"Thanks, honey," Jodi said.

Claire continued looking at me. "I'm so glad you and Jodi are friends. I know she's been lonely here. She had a good many friends in Denver. Of course, a few took advantage of her and proved not to be so great."

I looked over at Jodi. I could imagine that her gentle nature could easily be taken advantage of. She simply shrugged like it didn't matter and took a bite of a marshmallow. A bit of the sticky sweetness clung to her lip. The urge to wipe it off with my finger surprised me. It didn't surprise me to see Claire do it and pop her finger in her mouth. I looked away. I didn't see her, but I *heard* Claire kiss Jodi. I assumed on the mouth. Jodi was smiling when I looked back over at her. But her shoulders were slumped, almost in defeat. Her body belied the look on her face. I saw it but was willing to bet Claire didn't. I was sure Claire didn't see the heart or magnificence of Jodi.

I had done my best to open my heart and my home to Claire without judgment. But there it was. I *was* judging her. I was judging her as unworthy. Unworthy of Jodi or her love.

"How's mine?" Andrew showed me his marshmallow, toasted brown on one side and burnt black on the other.

"Looks great to me. Your mom says you play lacrosse."

"Yeah. We had our last game already."

"Oh. I would have liked to see you play."

"We lost. Did you ever play sports?"

"Nope. I was more into cheerleading than playing."

"That's cool," Andrew said. "When I get to high school I might play football. They get the cheerleaders." He wolfed down his marshmallow and proceeded to put another one on his stick. "Mom," he said to Jodi. "Next time you go get your hair cut, can I come and get mine cut too?"

"Of course," she said. She looked over at me and smiled. It warmed my heart.

The kids seemed to have a good time and I really liked having them and Jodi over. Claire I could tolerate for Jodi's sake.

Jodi helped me clean up while the kids and Claire continued to enjoy the fire.

"I can't believe how much Andrew talked to you tonight," Jodi said. "He hasn't said that much to me in the last month."

"He's a good kid," I told her. "We'll have to do this again sometime."

"I would like that."

Annie came into the kitchen with the bag of marshmallows. "We have some left," she said. "Where should I put them?"

"Thanks so much for helping, Annie. Do you want to take them home?" I looked at Jodi. "If it's okay with your mom."

"Can I, Mom?"

Jodi nodded. "Sure."

Annie gave me a tight hug. "Thanks. I had so much fun tonight."

"Me too."

Jodi wrapped her arms around both of us. "Group hug."

I didn't know exactly what it was about Jodi, but there was something that got under my skin and went right to my heart.

Jodi

I kissed both kids good-bye and gave them each a tight hug. These were the only times Andrew let me kiss him anymore. I brushed away a tear that somehow managed to disobey my order not to cry.

"You guys have a great time with your dad. Grandma's going to come and get you next week so you can spend time with her too."

Andrew rolled his eyes. "We know, Mom. You've told us ten times."

"I did not. I've been counting and it's only been nine."

I went over a list of things in my head that I'd wanted to make sure I told them, trying to figure out if there was anything I missed. Don't talk to anyone they didn't know—Andrew, keep an eye on your little sister—Don't spend the emergency money I gave you on anything foolish—Dad will be there waiting for you when you get off the plane.

I figured I had covered everything—at least three times. I gave them each another hug when they called for their flight to start boarding. I walked them to the line and watched them go down the hallway to their plane. Annie turned and waved just before they were out of sight. I let a few tears roll down my cheeks before brushing them away.

That quote from *A Tale of Two Cities*, "It was the best of times, it was the worst of times," came to mind. I missed my kids when they were gone for the summer, but it meant I got more alone time with Claire, and the tension in the house between her and the kids was temporarily gone.

I hung around the airport watching out the window until the plane taxied down the runway and out of sight. I sent a silent prayer and boatload of positive energy out for their safety and headed out to the parking lot.

Claire was still at work when I got home. I set the groceries I had picked up, along with the bottle of wine and flowers, on the kitchen table and went to let Tess out.

By the time Claire walked in the side door that led to the garage I was just putting the finishing touches on our dinner. I had two glasses of Claire's favorite wine poured and fresh flowers on the table.

"What's all this?" Claire asked.

I kissed her on the mouth. "This…" I waved my hands toward the table. "Is a romantic dinner to celebrate the first night of some much needed alone time."

"Nice. I'm just going to run upstairs to change."

I lit the candles on the table and dimmed the lights.

Claire came back down in record time and took her place at the table. "Wow. This is nice," she said. "I like it when it's just you and me."

We enjoyed a quiet dinner together catching up on each other's day, and Claire went to relax in front of the television while I cleaned up.

Later that night, I didn't bother with my pajamas and slipped under the sheets naked. I slid close to Claire and kissed her. I was aiming for her mouth, but she turned her head at the last second and my kiss landed on her cheek. I aimed again and this time found my target. But my target wasn't as willing to kiss me back as I had planned. We'd been through this before—a lot. I knew that in the past when I wasn't in the mood for sex, it sometimes only took a little coaxing to get me there. I often thought the same would hold true for Claire. I pushed on with my attempt at lovemaking. I found the soft skin of her stomach underneath her pajama top. As quickly as I started caressing her, her hand was on top of mine stopping its progression.

"Come on," I whispered in my most seductive voice. "We're all alone. It's just you and me."

"I'm really tired," she said. Her usual excuse. But I guess that was slightly better than the times she totally ignored my advances as if I wasn't even there. Those times I felt like crawling under a rock, but I usually just rolled over to my side of the bed and wished I was as invisible as she made me feel.

I decided to push just a bit harder—something I almost never did after being rejected. "Tomorrow's Saturday, sweetie. You can sleep in and make up for any sleep you lose tonight. I promise to make it worth your while." I moved in closer and planted tiny kisses down her neck.

She twisted just enough to let me know that she wanted me to stop. I did and without another word I got up and put my pajamas on. I crawled back into bed, being very conscious of staying on my own side.

"Good night," Claire said as if nothing had just transpired.

"Night," I said with my back toward her.

I could hear her reach for the television remote on her nightstand. The *Law and Order* repeat blared into the silence of the room. I put my pillow over my head to drown out the sound and my feelings of rejection.

The next morning, I needed to get out of the house for a while. After Claire's rejection, I didn't feel like spending time with her. I wanted to leave, but I didn't want her to know I was mad at her. Baggage from my childhood. I wasn't allowed to be mad in my father's presence. Ironic, since most of the time when I was mad during my childhood, I was mad at him. "Put a smile on your face," he would say. I would plaster that fake smile on long enough to be able to retreat to my room and away from him. Funny what we carried over from childhood. Thank God he had mellowed as he aged.

"I need to do some running around," I told her. "I have to go get some supplies for a sign order." It was the truth. I didn't need them until next week, but now was as good a time as any to get them. I was hoping she wouldn't offer to go with me. She didn't.

I gave her a chaste kiss good-bye and headed out to my car. I was almost to the store when my cell phone rang. A quick glance told me it was Beth. I stuck my Bluetooth in my ear and pressed the button.

"Hey there."

"Hi. I have a question for you."

"Shoot."

"Where can I get some of those fire starter sticks you mentioned? I thought it might make it easier using the fire pit."

"I'm out running errands," I told her. "I can stop and get you some. Will you be home in about an hour if I come by with it?" I hoped she'd say yes. I really wanted to see her. This was the perfect excuse. I calculated in my mind the best way to get to Home Depot from where I was.

"You don't have to do that. I'm sure you're busy."

"It's no problem. I don't have anything pressing I need to do today." I certainly didn't want to go home and spend time with Claire. I would much rather spend the rest of my day with Beth. I was assuming that she would be free to spend it with me. I loved the fact that she wasn't dating anyone and had no one she needed to account to. Please say I can come over, I thought. There was no way I could actually *tell* her how much I wanted that. It was a fine line between the crush I felt for her and making sure she didn't find out. "What do you think? It won't take me long to get them and get them to you."

"If you're sure it's not a problem."

I pulled into someone's driveway to turn around. Home Depot was in the other direction. "Not a problem at all. I'll be there shortly." I was about to say good-bye.

"Did you eat lunch? I can make us something when you get here."

Yes! I forced myself to keep my voice even—to keep the excitement out of it. "That would be great. See you soon." I hit the end button on my phone and tossed it on the seat next to me.

Beth

Sometimes I didn't know how to take Jodi's kindness. I appreciated it. That's for sure. But I knew she had been taken advantage of in her life by people who used her. She tried to hide her past hurt over it, but I knew it was there. The last thing I ever wanted to do was use Jodi or worse yet, hurt her. Jodi had become much more than just a good friend to me. She was my best friend. But even that didn't seem adequate enough. I searched for the right words in my mind to describe how I felt about her, but none came. I knew how I felt when I was with her. Those words flowed effortlessly through my mind. Happy. Thankful. Peaceful. Loved. Appreciated. Special. I liked how easy it was to talk to her. To be with her. I had never had a friend before that I felt so connected to. I think she felt it too. She went out of her way to spend time with me. At first, I thought maybe she felt sorry for me, being a single mom with no partner in my life. Funny how I used that word sometimes instead of what fit for me in the past—boyfriend, husband.

Knowing Jodi somehow equalized things in my mind, if that even made sense. Her relationship with her partner was no less real than any I would have had with a man. Claire. She was nowhere near Jodi's caliber. Their hearts didn't seem to match. I wasn't sure Claire even had one. I respected Jodi's choice for a life partner, but that didn't mean I had to think Claire was good enough for her. She wasn't. I couldn't quite understand why Jodi couldn't see it.

Jodi deserved to be loved deeper and treated better than Claire seemed capable of. I realized I didn't like seeing them together. Didn't like seeing them kiss good-bye or hug. Didn't like the way Claire rested her hand on Jodi's knee. The word *jealous* popped into my mind but was quickly erased. That was just plain ridiculous. There was nothing to be jealous of. I just wanted my friend to be happy. That was it. And I had heard Jodi say enough things about Claire—hell, I had witnessed enough things to know that Jodi wasn't really happy with Claire. At least I didn't think she was. Jodi never came right out and said that. And she stayed. Stayed with the woman who didn't treat her good enough. Why was that?

I also wondered what I had in the house to make for lunch when Jodi got here. Jodi. The thought of her made me smile and brought a lightness to my being. I certainly did like spending time with her. No one could make me laugh like she did. That's what I think I loved most about her. The word struck me. Love. I tossed it around in my mind. Love. Did I love her? Of course, I did. She was my friend. I loved other friends. Maybe not like this though. Love.

I turned it over again. Wait a minute. Love. Was I *in love* with her? No. I was straight. A hundred percent, perfectly straight. Straight women didn't fall in love with other women. That's not the way it worked. I searched my mind for any indication of anything like this happening to me before. I needed to sit. I eased myself down on the end of the couch and scratched my head. That was something I never realized I did when I was thinking until Jodi pointed it out. She noticed a lot of stuff about me that no one else ever did.

Maybe that was it. I just felt she was special because she paid attention. She was a lesbian. She paid attention to other women. My first—only—lesbian friend. Sure, it would feel different. I paid attention to her as well. I could tell how she was feeling simply by looking at her face or the way her shoulders rolled forward…or the toss of her head…or…so apparently, she wasn't the only one paying attention.

I've heard stories of people who knew they were gay from a young age. Jodi had told me that she started having crushes on girls in seventh grade. Patty Gorman, my best friend in middle school—no. No crush there. The other girls in cheerleading in high school—again nothing. Anywhere? Any indication that this would even be possible for me? No. You didn't wake up one day and go from being straight to being in love with another woman.

Was I in love with her? I asked myself again. I didn't really want to know the answer. The possibility of it was frightening. What would it say about me? Would that make me gay? What would my mother think if I was gay? Would she be mad? Being gay didn't work in my world. This was just stupid. I wasn't gay. That much I knew. But I couldn't definitely answer *no* to the question about whether I was in love with Jodi. I gathered up the feeling and the fear surrounding it and stuffed it into that secret compartment in my heart where I put everything I couldn't or wouldn't face—the grief from my father's death—the fear I felt at the prospect of being a single mother at seventeen—the stress of opening my own business—and now any undesired feeling for another woman. It would be safe there. Safe from the world. Safe from myself. Whether I was in love with her or not, I didn't have to think about it. I would never act on it so there was no need to really face it or figure it out. With the problem safely tucked away, I got up and went into the kitchen to figure out lunch.

Jodi

I considered telling Beth about what happened with Claire last night but decided against it. I loved Claire and wanted Beth to like her. I had the feeling Beth wasn't crazy about her, and this information would have made her like her even less.

I forced a smile, but it turned genuine as soon as Beth opened the door.

"Hey."

"Hey yourself," I answered. "I brought you a present." I handed her the bag of fire starters.

She put her hand to her chest. "Oh my. You shouldn't have." She feigned a southern accent. "Why, you are just so kind."

"My pleasure."

"Come on in." She stepped out of the way so I could pass. She smelled like vanilla and cinnamon. "What do I owe you?"

"Nothing. They were free."

She set them on the coffee table as we passed through the living room. "Yeah, right."

"All right, they weren't free. But I stole them so they didn't cost me anything."

"You're just too funny."

"Feed me lunch and we'll call it even."

"Deal." She led the way to the dining room. The table was set for two.

"Where's Maddie?"

"Out with friends, of course. Sit." She pointed at the chair across from her.

It shouldn't have made a difference, but I was glad it was just her and me. I told her about the kids leaving and how I felt about it.

"Gives you and Claire some alone time. That must be nice."

I nodded. Against my will, the details of last night and the lack of sex in my relationship came flooding out of my mouth as tears spilled from my eyes. Beth was on her feet in seconds with her arms around me. Her hug was warm and comforting.

"I'm sorry," I said.

"For what? For having feelings?"

"For ruining lunch."

"Stop it. You didn't ruin anything. As soon as I saw the tears, I moved the sandwiches out of the way." She sat back down and held up a plate. "See, all dry."

"Good reflexes." I wiped my eyes with a napkin.

"Reflexes extraordinaire you might say."

A giggle bubbled out of me. "Thank you."

"For what?"

"For making me laugh."

"Anytime," she said. "Anytime."

Beth

I turned the open/closed sign in the salon window around and unlocked the door. Cindy came in followed by Al Ferguson. I was surprised that his mother wasn't with him. A quick glance at the schedule book told me he didn't have an appointment.

"Hello, Mr. Ferguson. What can we do for you today?" I gave my best customer service smile.

"Al. Please."

"Al. What can I do for you?" I repeated.

"I was wondering…" He paused. "I was wondering," he started again. "If I could take you out to dinner some time."

I was taken aback. I hadn't been asked out in a long time. I felt like I was stumbling over my words. "Um…well…a…yes. Yes, that would be very nice." He seemed like a nice enough guy. He certainly treated his mother well. That surely was a good thing.

A smile took over his face. "Yes?"

I nodded.

"That's great. Friday? Would Friday work for you?"

I ran my schedule through my head. "Yes. I'm here till six."

"Should I pick you up here?"

I nodded. "Six thirty?"

"Perfect," he said. "Wonderful." He walked to the door. "See you on Friday." With a wave, he was gone.

"Nice looking guy." My sister walked in as Al walked out.

"Hi, Jen. Whatcha' doing here?"

"Hopefully, getting a haircut. I figured third time would be the charm. Do you have time?"

"You're in luck. Go ahead and have a seat. Let me finish setting up and I'll be right there."

I unlocked the register, counted the drawer, and turned the answering machine off. I had just draped the cape around my sister's neck when she looked at me in the mirror.

"So, your friend," she started. "Jodi."

I grabbed the spray bottle from the counter. "What about her?"

"She's gay, isn't she?"

I stopped spraying water onto Jen's hair. "What?"

"She mentioned someone named Claire calling on her lunch hour. Is that her wife?"

I felt the heat rise to my cheeks. "Partner." There. I said it and the world didn't stop. What the hell was wrong with me?

"I thought she gave off a gay vibe."

I continued wetting her hair. "What are you talking about?"

"You know the people at church wouldn't approve of your friendship?"

I turned her chair around so she was facing me. "Jodi is the kindest person I know."

She put her hands up. "I'm not saying it. I don't have a problem. I'm glad you have a friend. I'm just warning you that it might be frowned upon."

"What the fuck kind of a Christian attitude is that?"

Jen burst out laughing. "What kind of Christian *language* is that?"

I turned her chair back around but kept eye contact in the mirror as I worked on her hair.

I was at a loss for words. Jodi had more heart than most of the people sitting in those church pews each Sunday. They could take their backward attitudes and stick it up their asses. But church was important to me, even if those people weren't. "I would appreciate it if you wouldn't say anything to anyone." I was ashamed of my words almost as soon as they were out of my mouth. No. I refused to be ashamed of Jodi. Of my friendship with her.

"I wonder—" Jen started to say.

"Scratch that," I told her. "Never mind. I don't care."

"Beth. Chill. It's not that big a deal."

But Jodi was a big deal to me.

Jodi

The kids had been gone most of the summer, and sex with Claire had happened only once in all that time. It seemed forced, almost robotic on her part. It made me wonder why I had even bothered trying.

I had dinner with Beth, Maddie, and Beth's mom a couple of times when Claire had to work late. I really enjoyed their company and Beth treating me like I was part of the family. She had been dating a man named Al for most of the summer. I had met him a few times and he seemed like a nice enough guy. For some reason, I didn't like it. I told myself it was because she had less time for me, but if I was being honest with myself it was probably more than that. I still loved Claire—with all my heart—but I spent so much time being angry at her lately that it made spending time with Beth all the better.

I opened a bottle of beer and brought it downstairs so I could work on a design for a new customer. Claire was at work and the house was quiet. Tess sat at my feet keeping me company.

I missed my kids. I missed Claire even though she hadn't really gone anywhere. Or maybe she had. Our relationship certainly wasn't what it used to be. But I was nowhere near ready to give up on it.

I had been working for a couple of hours when Tess picked her head up. She heard the sound the same time that I did.

"Hey, babe. I'm home." It was Claire.

"Up in a few."

I saved my work on the computer, shut everything down, and headed up the stairs.

Tess beat me up and greeted Claire with lick on the hand and a wildly wagging tail.

"Okay, enough," Claire told her. "Hi, hon," she said to me. "I just came home to change. Remember I have that office party for Milly. Today was her last day. Retiring after twenty-five years. You're still welcome to come with me."

I didn't want to. I didn't know those people, and even though Claire did her best to include me, I still felt like an outsider. "I appreciate that. I'm sure you'll have more fun without me."

"Suit yourself." She grabbed her briefcase and headed upstairs to change.

I opened the refrigerator to figure out what leftovers I could warm up for myself later for dinner. The ravioli and meatballs from two days ago would have to do.

Claire came down wearing a fresh pair of jeans and T shirt. It was obviously a casual gathering. She kissed me on the cheek and headed out the door.

My phone rang as I was putting my dinner in the microwave. It was Beth. "Hey."

"Hi. Whatcha doing?"

"Warming up leftovers. I lead a very exciting life."

"I was hoping you were free to see a movie with me. Maybe catch dinner if you haven't eaten yet. And it sounds like you haven't. But I don't want to interfere with your exciting leftover plans."

I pulled my plate from the microwave. "I might be persuaded to give up my leftovers for dinner and a movie."

"Oh yeah. And what would it take to persuade you?"

"Just ask me nice." I smiled at our exchange.

"Pretty please, would you go to dinner and a movie with me?"

I wrapped the plate of food in plastic wrap and stuck it back in the fridge. "Okay. Stop begging. I'll go."

A half hour later, I was sitting across from Beth laughing my head off with a drink in my hand.

"So, the kids should be back next week, right?" Beth asked.

"Yep. I talk to them a few times a week, but it's not the same. Their dad is good to them, but I'll be glad to have them back."

"I'm sure."

"How's it going with Al?" I asked, both needing to know and not really wanting the answer.

"Great. He treats me really good. Always buying me flowers and gifts. I've never really had that kind of attention from anyone before."

"I'm glad," I said, doing my best to mean it. What the hell was wrong with me? Of course, I should be glad my friend had such a wonderful guy. I was. Wasn't I?

Beth

My mind was still on Jodi and our evening together the next day as I walked up to Al's door. It was great to be able to spend time with her. I really missed her. I knew it was my fault I hadn't seen her as much lately. I'd been spending more and more time with Al. I liked him and it made sense. I pushed the fact that I would have rather spent my time with Jodi deep in that secret compartment in my heart where I didn't have to think about it or face it.

I knocked on Al's door and he opened it with a smile across his face. "Hi, sweetie pie," he said. He pulled me into a tight hug. "Come on in. Mom's at daycare. We have the place to ourselves."

We had been dating almost two months and hadn't yet slept together. Part of it was that we both had other people living with us. Sleepovers just weren't practical at this point. My work schedule kept most of my days full. Al was a stockbroker so his schedule was pretty much his own. I took the day off for the precise reason of having sex. It was time. Al had been more than patient.

It felt good to be held, to be touched, to be wanted. It had been way too long. As I lay in his arms afterward, naked, vulnerable, momentarily satisfied, he whispered in my ear.

"I love you." His quiet declaration took me by surprise.

I searched my mind and my heart to see if I could return his sentiment. I wasn't sure. I felt I was on the edge of such feelings but wasn't quite there. "I love you too," I heard myself say. I wasn't sure where the words were coming from. But there they were.

He pulled me in for a kiss which deepened quickly and became much more. After our second round of lovemaking, I told myself maybe I did love him.

"Will you stay for dinner?" Al asked me as we scrambled to put our clothes back on. He had to pick his mother up from her adult daycare. We had lost track of time and he was cutting it close.

"I would love to, but Maddie will be home and I promised her we would order pizza from her favorite place tonight." She had, at my insistence, gotten a summer job. Working as a counselor at our local park seemed to suit her well, and her general attitude adjustment had been a welcome change. I was sure the fact that I let her buy a used car and covered the insurance on it contributed to the change as well.

"Have her come here. Order the pizza and we can all eat together. It won't take me long to go get Mom."

Maddie did seem to like Al. We hadn't actually talked about it, but I'm sure she was glad I had someone taking so much of my attention.

"Sure. We can do that. I'll give her a call."

"Make yourself at home. I'll be back in a flash." Al kissed me one more time and headed out the door. I made my way to the living room. Al and his mom lived in Pittsford, an affluent, most would say rich, neighborhood, and the house reflected the area. The large two-story home sported five bedrooms, three full baths, and a fully finished basement. Al had moved in with his mother when her memory problems proved to be dementia and it became obvious that she could no longer care for herself. The seemingly selfless act raised him up several notches in my mind.

A quick call to Maddie and another to the pizza place and my tasks were done. With time to kill, I pulled up the contact list on my phone and hit Jodi's name. She answered on the second ring.

"Insane asylum. Main nut speaking. How can I help you?"

I laughed. "That bad, huh?"

"It was. It's looking up now that I'm talking to you."

"What's going on?"

"Oh, just struggling with a design for a very picky client. No biggy. I'll hit on something he likes. What's going on with you?"

"I'm hanging at Al's waiting for him to get home with his mother." I left out the fact that we had made love for the first time. I shared almost everything with Jodi. I wasn't sure why I didn't share that. "I don't want to interrupt your work. Should I let you get back to it?"

"Hell no. I could use the break. And talking to you is not only a break, it's a treat."

I smiled. Talking to Jodi always made me feel good. I made a mental note to do it more. No more neglecting this wonderful person on the other end of the phone.

Jodi

The kids had been home and back in school for the last four months. It was good to have them home, and Christmas was just around the corner. One of my favorite times of the year. I had made a handful of new friends in Rochester, but Beth had remained my closest friend and confidant. Things with Claire were going good. Maybe *good* was an overstatement. Smoothly was more accurate. Sex was still a rare occurrence, but I was doing research on low sex drives and the causes and was more optimistic that maybe we could fix the problem. Although, I was the only one who seemed to think it was problem. Claire seemed perfectly fine having sex every six months or so. Even that seemed like it was too much for her.

I put the thoughts of Claire aside and concentrated on my Christmas list. I had the kids pretty much figured out. Annie had gotten her own iPad from Claire and me for her birthday in September. She was a budding artist and writer. She loved playing around with the drawing and writing apps. A really nice, aka expensive, stylist pencil, along with a wireless keyboard would certainly help her up her game. Andrew was into video games much more than I would have liked, but he wanted the latest version of *Super Mario Odyssey*, and seeing it wasn't violent we got it for him. Claire and I had agreed not to go overboard with gifts for each other so she was getting a new wallet. It was Beth I was stuck on. I wanted to get her something nice. Something that showed I cared, but not something that showed I cared too much.

She and Al were still going strong. I'm sure he would be getting her something spectacular. He was always very generous with her. Her jewelry collection had grown by leaps and bounds since they started dating.

I opened my computer to look for ideas for the perfect Christmas gift for her. I was still scouring the internet when she called.

"Speak of the devil," I said into the phone when I answered.

"Were you speaking of the devil or am I the devil of which you speak?"

"I've always thought of you more as an angel than a devil."

"Good to know. This angel would like to know if you are free for lunch tomorrow."

I knew Beth's life was often a juggling act between her daughter, her business, and Al, but I appreciated the fact that Beth always seemed to make time for us to be together.

"For you? I'll make sure I'm free. Just tell me where and when."

"Twelve thirty? Benny's by the salon?"

"You got it." I found myself looking forward to it, more than I was willing to admit to myself.

❖

I slid into the booth across from Beth.

A huge smile lit up her face. "Al asked me to marry him."

Her words hit me square in the chest. I forced a smile. Of course, he asked her. Why wouldn't he? Beth was a catch. Beautiful. Kind. Genuine. A rare find. If I was single and she was gay I would have pursued her with all I was worth. She deserved the best in life and Al seemed like a good guy. I wanted her to be happy. I truly did. "What did you say?"

"I said yes, of course." I looked at the hand she held up. It sported a large diamond ring.

Bigger than I knew I could ever afford to give her. Stop it, I told my brain. You will never be buying her a ring. She's marrying someone else. She will never be yours. Besides, I had Claire. I loved Claire. I built a life with Claire. But Beth. What was it about Beth? She smiled at me. The answer to my question was in her smile. It was pure. Her whole being radiated with it. My feelings for her couldn't be summed up in words. Yes, there was love, but it went far beyond that. I knew my feelings transcended this life. They reached back to before we were born and they reached into the future further than anything I could comprehend. Stop it. Stop it. Stop it, I thought. Be happy for her. I stood and put my arms out to her. She extracted herself from the booth and I pulled her into a tight hug. I did my best to ignore her heart beating against mine and the way my blood ran hotter when she was this close.

Beth

The last couple of months were a whirlwind of activity. I would have been happy to wait a year and plan the wedding a little at a time. Al wanted to get married right away. He rented the venue, planned the meal, and help me pick out the invitations. Maddie was my maid of honor, Jen and Jodi were my bridesmaids. They all looked so beautiful. Especially Jodi in the peach colored full-length gown we had picked out together for her to wear. My heart skipped a beat when she tried it on and did a twirl in front of me. I took her shoulders and turned her toward the mirror on the other side of the room. Her skin beneath my fingertips was warm. Too warm. My fingers ached to move over that soft skin. To caress her. I brought my attention back to the task at hand and the fact that I was getting married.

"You like it?" she asked me, catching my eye in the mirror.

I like you, I thought. Too much. I like you too much. I was getting married and my thoughts were on Jodi. Her beauty. Her warmth. Her.

"Beth?"

I brought my thoughts back to the dress. "Very much. You?"

She turned around until we were face-to-face. She was so close to me. "Beth?"

I was flustered by her close proximity.

"Beth?" she repeated.

I took a step back and turned around.

Her hands were on my shoulders briefly before she wrapped her arms around me. "Beth," she said one more time, this time directly in my ear. It sent a shiver down my spine. "Are you okay?"

I closed my eyes and swallowed hard. "Just nerves." I pulled out of her warm, comforting embrace.

"Are you sure you want to do this?"

I'm sure. I'm sure I need to let go of these feelings. They rose without my permission. My recent attempts to stuff them back into that secret box proved unsuccessful. I turned around to face Jodi. I got lost in her eyes for a split second before answering. "It's just nerves," I repeated. "I'll be fine."

And I was. The wedding went off without a hitch. Everyone told me how beautiful I looked in my long white dress. Al looked so handsome in his tux. His mother couldn't attend due to a recent fall and a stay in the hospital. I offered to postpone, but Al wouldn't hear of it. She wouldn't remember it anyway, he reminded me.

Jodi gave me a rose quartz in the shape of a heart. It was wrapped in velvet and tucked into a handmade wooden box. The note included said:

For my best friend,
This rose quartz is a symbol of unconditional love. It opens the heart, increases self-love, friendship, and healing. May it bring you inner peace and harmony in everything you do for all your life.
All my love,
Jodi

We started our life as a married couple in Jamaica on our honeymoon. The warm sand and sunshine were just what I needed. My texts and pictures to Jodi were frequent. I wanted to share the experience with her. I set the rose quartz heart in the sand and took pictures of it with the ocean in the background. I texted the best one to her.

Hey. She texted back. *Don't lose that on the beach.*

Lol. I won't. It's too important to me.

I can't believe you brought it on your honeymoon.

Of course I did. I'm going to put it in my nightstand by my bed when I get home. I want to keep it close by.

"Texting Jodi, again?" Al asked, sitting in the lounge chair next to me.

I felt like I had been caught cheating. She was just a friend I told myself, but I knew better. My feelings for her were too strong. I looked at Al and closed my phone. "Last time. I promise." It was a promise I intended to keep. How could I look Al in the eye and be thinking about Jodi? It was never going to work.

That was the third message Jodi left me. I looked at it but didn't pick it up either to answer the phone when it rang or to listen to the voice mail. How could I tell her that I couldn't see her anymore—couldn't be around her? How could I make a new marriage work and love her at the same time? I pushed my feelings for her way down into the bottom of my heart where the moths and rust couldn't ruin it. I locked it up tight and put the key where no one would ever find it.

If I saw her or even talked to her on the phone, I knew that lock wouldn't be able to contain my feelings and I couldn't trust my mouth not to let the truth tumble out. I couldn't risk that.

Jodi

Four Years Later

I woke up the morning of my forty-fifth birthday and thought, *Where the hell am I*? It wasn't that I physically didn't know where I was. I was in the house I shared with my partner of nine years tucked away on that cozy little cul-de-sac in the suburbs. I would have called her my lover, but we hadn't made love in well over a year. I'd spent so much time trying to get our love life back. I wooed her with flowers and compliments and romance. I gave her space to figure out that she missed that part of me, of us. I begged, I pleaded, I cried. I gave up trying. On the rare occasion that she would toss me a bone, I was made to feel like she was doing me a favor.

Lovemaking became stiff, forced, robotic. My kisses were unanswered and she performed as if following a script. She would touch my cheek twice, move down to the breasts giving each one thirty seconds of attention, run her fingers across my stomach and down to the pleasure center, stroke and insert. Not wet yet? Oh well, continue anyway so I can't say we never make love any more. And oh yeah, don't let her body get too close to me while she's doing it.

I would spend months wanting her, needing her, and when I finally got her for several minutes I would wonder why I had bothered trying. Her small offering left me feeling even more empty and alone than before.

Our love life became the pattern for our everyday existence, and I watched her move away from me and what we shared as if in slow motion. My arms reaching out for her to keep her close but catching nothing but air.

Did I still love her? I didn't know. I still cared about her. A piece of me still wanted her, still wanted her to want me.

I came from a family where you stayed together through thick and thin, good times and bad, or any other cliché you cared to throw in there. I was an only child—never daring enough to cause trouble to get noticed, I was quiet and shy—the *good* kid. I had witnessed, through closed doors, my parents fighting from time to time. I could rarely make out the muffled words, and sometimes the tension in the house would last for days, but in the end, they would always come back together, stronger than they were before. I learned at a young age that fighting with the one you loved was normal and could even be good. I learned you just needed to stick it out for a few days.

My days turned into months and then into years. I was waiting for us to come back together and be stronger. Only this wasn't really fighting. I think both people needed to care in order to fight. This was more like Claire was pulling away, inch by painful inch, and I was powerless to stop her. For a long time, I thought maybe there was something wrong with me. Something I needed to figure out and do different in order for her to want me. That had been a theme in my life—there's something wrong with me.

If Claire didn't act like she loved me, didn't want me, didn't want to touch me—there's something wrong with me. But I'd come to the conclusion that it was not me. The only thing wrong with me was that I hadn't drawn up enough courage to actually walk out the door—until the day I did.

BETH

This wasn't the way it was supposed to be. I did everything I could to make sure my marriage would succeed. Hell, I had even lost my best friend to make sure my feelings for her didn't get in the way. And what did he do? He fucking cheated on me. It was just a few times he said. It was over he said. He still loved me. He begged for my forgiveness.

I'm not sure he ever would have told me about it had I not found the charges on the credit card statement. Awfully stupid of him not to use cash to pay for hotel rooms and to buy his mistress gifts.

He agreed to counseling with the pastor of our church. I was in the process of forgiving him. It was taking some time. I let him back into the bedroom but found myself sleeping on the edge of the bed in an effort to stay away from him. I still couldn't let him touch me. Not the way he had touched *her*.

People make mistakes. I told myself that again and again. I didn't want my marriage to fail. If I could just forgive him, we could get past this. But it wasn't that simple. Forgiveness didn't get back the trust. Didn't get back what we lost. No, not what we *lost*—what he threw away. What he tore apart, waded into a ball, and stomped on. No getting back to where we were—or maybe we were never really there. I just didn't know anymore.

To the rest of the world, nothing had changed. I went to work, bought groceries from Wegmans, and went to family functions. No one knew. No one except my mother.

"Men will be men," she said to me. "It's what they do."

That wasn't good enough for me. "Forsaking all others," he had said in church, in front of me, in front of a hundred and fifty people. In front of God. But he hadn't forsaken her. He had fucked her.

Jodi

I hadn't seen Beth in more than four years. She had slowly and silently slipped out of my life. I chalked it up to her new marriage and a husband who didn't want to share her. It hurt but I understood. At least that's what I told myself. I didn't want to hate her. I loved her too much for that. I figured it would be better—healthier for me and my relationship with Claire—if I let Beth go without a fight. When she started to slip away, I let her. But the end of my relationship with Claire was upon me, and what I needed most was a friend. Not just any friend. I needed Beth.

It took me a week to gather up enough courage to call her. I had no idea if she would even answer. I was a little surprised when she did. She seemed genuinely happy to hear from me. We made plans for lunch the following day.

I woke when the sun came up. Elation and a bit of anxiety wouldn't let me sleep any longer. A lot had changed since I had last seen Beth. I had my own apartment—tiny, but mine. My business was now located in a small storefront on Main Street.

My mom had died three years ago and my dad six months later. I was swallowed up by grief for a long while, but that had settled down to a dull ache. Andrew was at boot camp, training to be a marine. He had joined against my strong objections. My ex-husband was all for it. "It will make a man out of him," he told me. The stress of it caused a cascade of stomach pains on a regular basis. I took up meditation as a path to relaxation. It wasn't helping as much as I had hoped.

Annie was fourteen and would soon be a freshman in high school. My kids were definitely growing up. My relationship was done, and I was feeling left behind. I wondered what life was like for Beth.

I tapped my foot in a steady rhythm. I had arrived a few minutes early and ordered a drink to steady my nerves. I wasn't quite sure what I was so nervous about. My anxiety bordered on fear. I was afraid the strength of my feelings for Beth would come rushing back. But I was more afraid they wouldn't. I was afraid Beth's feelings for me had changed. That we wouldn't be able to find our way back to friendship. If they'd changed would I know it? Would I be chasing after a friendship that didn't exist anymore?

I looked up from the menu in time to see Beth walk through the door. My breath caught in my throat. There was no denying the feelings were still there. I just had to be sure I could keep them under control. I was surprised that I had almost forgotten how beautiful she was. During the years we were out of touch I thought mostly about the pain of missing her. I forget the actual *her* I was missing. Because that was who I loved. The actual *her*.

I was on my feet as Beth approached the table. Her face lit up with a huge grin. There she was. My friend. She was back in the blink of an eye. The hug she gave me confirmed it.

The conversation flowed as if no time had passed. We touched on every subject but the one that had separated us four years ago. Why had we lost touch and drifted apart?

I broached the subject choosing my words carefully. Not wanting to place blame. Not wanting to put another wedge between us.

"Four years ago, I felt like you pulled back and away from me. It was shortly after you got married. I let you do it without much of a fight," I said, just pointing out the facts as I saw them.

She averted her eyes for a few seconds and then brought them back to me. She swallowed hard. "Did it ever occur to you that I did that because I had feelings for you?"

What? No. That never occurred to me. How could that be true? How could I not figure that out? Everything pointed to the opposite. She pulled away because she didn't want to be my friend, not because she wanted to be my lover. "Wait a minute," I said. "What are you saying?" I obviously didn't understand.

"I had feelings for you. I found it very hard to be around you and not touch you."

"Why didn't you ever tell me?" The whole room had taken on a surreal feeling. All the time I wanted her, she wanted me back?

"I wasn't going to be the reason you broke up with Claire. You loved her. I wanted to honor that. And then I married Al. There was no sense telling you when we were both with other people."

"When you say it was hard for you not to touch me…you mean everything? Could you have had sex with me?" Did this mean she wasn't straight after all? I was confused.

"Oh yes," she said. "Without a doubt. But it was only you."

"What do you mean?"

"You are the only woman I've ever been attracted to. The only one I've ever had those feelings for. I don't know what that means. I don't know what that makes me. I've never told anyone this. And to be quite honest…" She paused for a very long moment. "The thought of it terrified me."

"Why?"

She hesitated, apparently choosing her words carefully. "You didn't frighten me. The thought I might be gay did."

I didn't have to ask why. It had frightened me for a long time. Beth was brought up in a strict religion. She still attended church regularly. I'm sure the thought was even harder for her than it had been for me.

"Why are you telling me now?" All the years of wanting her, all that time thinking my feelings were mine alone and now this. It was hard to wrap my head around.

"Because you deserve the truth."

She said she *had* had feelings for me. Did that mean those feelings were gone? I had assumed all of these years of not seeing her made my feelings fade into the background. Maybe the same thing happened for her. She was still married. I assumed she still loved Al.

She had mentioned there had been some problems, but she also said they were trying to work it out.

Beth

It was hard for me to admit my feelings to Jodi, but she deserved the truth. She deserved to know why I had to walk away. I hadn't planned on it, but when she brought up the fact that I had pulled away, it just came pouring out. I had missed her dearly the last several years. There were times I picked up my phone and stared at her contact information with my finger hovering over the dial button. But in the end, I never pressed it. My marriage had to be my number one priority. My feelings for Jodi would just get in the way.

Maddie was living in my house, working part-time and going to Monroe Community College. She had her life on track. I was proud of her. I was living in Al's house. His mother never recovered from her fall and she died in the hospital shortly after we returned from our honeymoon. Al seemed to take it well.

I attended church every Sunday and Al accompanied me most weeks. When I found out about his affair I insisted he start counseling with our minister. He agreed. He upped his efforts to win back my affections with flowers and expensive gifts. They didn't make a difference. I knew only time and honesty would heal my heart. I vowed to give him the chance to prove himself.

Seeing Jodi again was wonderful. I believed my feelings for her were in check. The time apart had helped me lock them away. I was sure we could be friends again. I wanted that almost as much as I wanted my marriage to work.

I was surprised that Jodi had left Claire. I knew she hadn't been totally happy with her, but I also thought she had enough love to stay, despite the fact that Claire didn't deserve her.

"How are you doing with the breakup?" I asked.

She took a long swig of her Manhattan before answering. "It took a lot for me to get to the place where I could leave. Part of it was fear. You know how hard it is running your own business. There can be dry spells where the money just doesn't come in."

I nodded.

The waitress took that moment to clear the dishes from our table. "Can I get you anything else? We have a wonderful dessert menu?"

Jodi ordered another drink. We both passed on dessert. She continued as soon as we were alone again. "I reached a point where I was willing to live in my car if I had to. I just couldn't stay any longer. The love was gone. It was torture being there."

"Oh, Jodi." I put my hand over hers but pulled it back again. I wasn't prepared for the tingle I felt touching her. If she noticed she gave no indication.

"Claire didn't want me to leave. Begged me to stay. Swore she would change."

"That didn't make a difference?"

"I had been telling her for years what my needs were. She wasn't willing to change during that time. I had given up trying. I didn't think she could change, or if she did I knew it would be short-lived."

"Do you need a place to stay? Money? Are you okay?" There was no way I could let her sleep in her car.

She shook her head. "No. I have an apartment. It isn't much, but it's mine. Annie is with her father in Denver for the summer."

The waitress returned with Jodi's drink, and left the bill on the table. I picked it up before Jodi had a chance to.

"Hey," she said, pointing at the check.

"I've got this."

"I didn't tell you that so you would feel sorry for me."

I glanced at the bill, slipped my credit card in the folder, and set it down out of Jodi's reach.

"Feel sorry for you? Never. You are the strongest, kindest woman I know. You'll land on your feet. I'm taking care of the bill today. I'll be ordering surf and turf next time, when it's your turn to pay."

She laughed. My heart warmed to the sound of it. I had missed her. Truly. Desperately. Missed her.

Jodi

Beth's words stayed with me over the next week and bounced around in my head like an out of control ping-pong ball. She had feelings for me. Could she still have them? I knew I still felt for her. She'd never told me because of Claire—didn't want to be the one to break us up. She had taken away my choice. I didn't know how she felt, so I couldn't choose her over Claire.

The more I thought about it, the more I thought there was a good chance I would have chosen her. I would still choose her. She took the high road. I wasn't sure I wanted to do the same. I wanted to tell her I returned her feelings. See if there was any chance she would choose me. Could I put her in that position? I didn't know.

I did know I didn't have to decide anything right away. The task at hand was to get ready to go over to her house. Al was out for the evening—some church counseling session Beth had said.

I went through several outfits before deciding on simple jeans and a T-shirt. I laughed when Beth opened the door and she was dressed almost identically.

She gave me a tight hug, which I didn't let go on too long, as much as I would have liked to. She led me to the large living room and sat on the couch next to me. The coffee table in front of us held an array of cheese, crackers, and other munchies.

"I made you a drink," she said, pointing to what looked like a Manhattan. "I can make you something different if you want."

I took a sip. "Nope. This is perfect."

She picked up her drink, which looked to be the same as mine. "To our friendship," she said and clinked her glass against mine. We both took a sip.

"I'm so glad you're back in my life," I told her.

"Me too." She smiled that smile. It went directly to my heart and wrapped it in warmth and want. I hadn't planned it, and I'm not sure I could have stopped it, but I leaned forward and kissed her. Kissed her full on the mouth for all I was worth. What's more is she kissed me back. Her tongue slipped into my mouth and took full possession.

I lost control of my hands and my fingers tangled in her hair and pulled her even closer to me. I felt a surge of wetness as my arousal rose. I had wanted this for so long. So long.

The back of Beth's hand skimmed across my breast and my nipple stood at full attention aching to be touched. Her hands were on my back, my neck, my shoulders. Without much conscious thought, I took her hand in mine and brought it to my chest. Without further prompting, her fingers kneaded my flesh. My breath caught in my throat.

I slipped a hand under her shirt and found my target. Her nipple responded and she let out a moan that I quickly swallowed up with my mouth. She leaned back, pulling me with her until I was lying on top of her. I adjusted my position and slipped a knee between her legs.

"Stop," she said, breaking the kiss.

I didn't have enough breath in my body to respond. I asked the question with my eyes.

"I can't do this."

I sat up, releasing the breast I had taken possession of.

She took several long moments to compose herself, taking deep breaths and letting them out with a large puff of air.

My eyes never left hers as she sat up and smoothed down her hair.

We sat like that for what seemed like an eternity but probably didn't last more than a minute.

"I shouldn't have—" I started.

"No. It's not you. I want this too." She took my hand. "I really do." She took another deep breath. She hadn't totally collected herself yet. "I don't want to cheat. I didn't tell you this, but Al had an affair."

I stroked the back of her hand. "Oh, Beth, I'm so sorry."

"I don't want to sink to his level. I don't want to cheat," she repeated. "I need time to think. To figure out what I want. What I need to do."

I didn't dare ask the question that tugged at my brain. Could she leave him for me? Would she?

She seemed to read my mind. "I vowed to let him redeem himself. To prove he was sorry and to make up for it. I need to decide what that means." She pointed from herself to me. "What this means."

I nodded, not sure what to say. I wanted her. She wanted me. Right now, that was all I needed to know.

She looked into my eyes. "Can you do that? Can you give me time?"

Of course. I could give her anything at this point. "Yes."

She ran a single finger across my cheek. The feeling went directly through me. It passed through my heart and settled squarely in my center. I wasn't sure I could continue to sit so close to her and not run my hands over her body.

I got up and moved the chair across from the couch.

"I'm so sorry," she said.

I put my hand up. "Stop. It's fine. I just need to catch my breath."

"Should we talk about this?"

I nodded, wanting her to start. I took a large gulp of my drink while I waited.

"I told you I had had feelings for you. I tried to bury them, but tonight they came out in full force. But what I'm not sure of are your feelings. You haven't been away from Claire that long. Did this... this..." She seemed at a loss for words.

"This happened," I said. "Because I have had feelings for you since soon after we met."

"But you were with Claire. You loved her."

I nodded. "I did. But..." Now it was me who was stumbling for words. "But that didn't stop me from falling for you. Maybe that's why I was so willing to let you slip out of my life. Because I didn't want those feelings to complicate my life with Claire."

She pushed a stray hair out of her face. "This isn't a rebound thing?"

"Not at all. I realized last week when we saw each other that my feelings hadn't changed." I moved back to the couch and took her hands in mine. I looked deep into her blue eyes. I swore I could see her soul—her very being—there. "Tell me your feelings for me haven't changed either? That kiss told me they haven't changed."

"Even telling you my feelings haven't changed makes me feel like I'm cheating."

I was willing to let her cheat. To cheat with me. What did that say about me—other than I wanted her. "Where do we go from here?"

"At the moment, we go nowhere. Jodi, I'm married."

It was a fact I didn't need—want—to be reminded of.

She dropped my hands. "It's up to you now. Can we be friends and not let this come between us?"

"Is there any chance at all for us?"

"I honestly don't know. I'm not ready to give up my marriage yet." She let out an exasperated sigh. "Oh, this is all so confusing."

The last thing I wanted to do was cause her any kind of discomfort. "Let's drop it for now. I can handle being friends. We aren't animals. Surely, we're capable of controlling our urges. And if we're not, well, I guess that says something." I would give her time to figure things out. Of course, I hoped she would choose me. Choose what we could be together. But I wouldn't push. She was too important to me. I didn't want to send her running again.

"Do you want me to go?" Please say no.

"No. Of course not. How about we put a movie on and just enjoy watching it together?"

It was a plan I could live with. I nodded.

She got up, grabbed the remote from the end table, and sat back down next to me. I resisted the urge to take her hand.

"What do you want to watch?" she asked me.

"How about some sappy lesbian movie?"

She laughed. It dispelled some of the tension coursing through the air. "How about a nice tame comedy?"

Okay. I could settle for that. For now.

Beth

Wow. Wow. Wow! That kiss wasn't expected. But what was more of a surprise was the way my body reacted. I was on fire with desire. Every fiber of my being vibrated with want. Want for Jodi.

Married. That word didn't seem to matter in that moment. It took everything I had to stop the kiss. Of course, I couldn't stop the wanting. The throbbing between my legs continued through most of the movie. It was all I could do not to let Jodi continue or worse yet, use my hand to reach the release my body screamed for. I managed to resist either option.

Jodi wanted me. Had wanted me for a long time. How easy it would be to give myself to her. But that damn word sprung up again. Married. I would not—could not—cheat. I had made a vow to him, to God. For better or worse. Yes, he had done the worse, but wasn't marriage meant to be forever?

I needed to stick it out. My heart wanted Jodi. The piece of paper in a frame that hung in our bedroom said I belonged to Al. There was no decision to be made here. I had made my decision when I walked down the aisle of that church and made my promises. I wasn't sure how I was going to do it, but I needed to tell Jodi. I just hoped I didn't lose her forever.

Jodi

"I need to work on my marriage," Beth said. She paused before adding, "For now."

"What exactly does 'for now' mean?" I asked, using air quotes.

She shook her head. "I don't know. I mean..." Beth got up from the chair she was sitting in across from me in my apartment. She sat next to me on the couch and took my hand. A surge of emotions filled me. Sadness for what she was telling me. Hope that "for now" meant her marriage would fail and she would come to me. Arousal at the physical contact.

"I mean," she went on, "I have to continue on the path I started with Al. I have to give it everything I have. I'm not sure I'm gay or bi or any other label. To be honest, those labels scare me. I'm just me and I have a husband.

I inhaled sharply. "So, you are choosing him over me?"

"It's not a choice. It's where I am right now. Married."

"What does that mean for us?"

"Jodi, I care about you. You are very special to me. Please don't doubt that. I want to work at being friends. Best friends. Do you think we can do that?"

Friends. The word never sounded so unsettling as it did in that moment. Could I do it? Could I push my feelings for her aside and settle for being friends? I had pushed them aside before. But this time it was different. I was no longer in love with Claire, and now I knew my feelings for Beth were returned.

If I didn't agree, I knew Beth wouldn't be able to stay in my life— and my life was so much better with her in it. If I did agree would I be opening myself up for a world of hurt?

I slowly nodded, giving the only answer I could live with. The words "for now" continued to circulate in my mind. There was still a chance. I could cling to that hope—for now.

We managed to pull it off for several months. Just being friends. My feelings for her didn't wane of course. They seemed to get stronger. The more we saw each other, the more time I wanted to spend with her. Her feelings, on the other hand, were hard to read. She was careful not to let me see anything more than friendship. Our hugs were short, she sat on the other side of the couch or across from me, always careful not to be too close.

I sat in my car tapping on the steering wheel. The fact that there were four cars in the driveway and in front of the house told me that the rest of Beth's dinner guests had already arrived. Seeing Beth's mother, sister, and daughter wasn't the problem. Sitting at the same table and watching Beth and Al played married couple was.

I gathered up my courage, grabbed the bottle of wine I had brought from the passenger seat, and headed up the sidewalk to the front door. Beth's sister, Jen, opened it almost as soon as I rang the bell.

"Hi, Jodi. It's so good to see you." She gave me a one-armed hug, holding a full glass of wine in her other hand. "Beth's in the kitchen. Come on in." She took my coat and hung it in the hall closet.

I made my way to the kitchen. "This is for you," I said when I saw Beth. I handed her the bottle of merlot.

"How nice." She gave me a tight but short-lived hug. I ignored the sensations it stirred. "I have some white wine already opened, but I can open this if you would prefer it."

"White works."

Beth's mom, Denise, came into the kitchen, followed by Maddie. "Looks like the party's in here. Hi, Jodi. How are you?"

I gave her and Maddie each a hug in turn. "Doing good. How are you?"

"Oh, you know. Hanging in there. Can't complain." She turned to Beth. "Honey, did you need any help?"

"I've got it, Mom. Why don't you take this tray out to the living room? You guys can snack while I put the finishing touches on dinner."

She handed her a platter filled with cheese and crackers. Maddie grabbed a piece of cheese as her grandmother passed and stuffed it into her mouth. She held up an empty wine glass. "Uncle Roger would like another," she told her mother.

Beth gestured to the bottle on the kitchen island. "And pour Jodi a glass too, please."

"Thanks," I said to Maddie, accepting the glass. I took a large sip.

Beth drained a pot of potatoes, added butter and milk, and proceeded to mash them. "I'm so glad you're here." She looked over at me and smiled.

I raised my glass without saying anything but returned the grin.

"If you want you can go out to the living room with everyone else and have some munchies."

"Okay if I just hang in here with you for a while?"

"Absolutely. I would love that."

"What do you want me to do?"

"Nothing. Just keep me company. Pull up a chair and relax."

I sat silently sipping my wine, watching Beth prepare the meal, hoping the wine would settle the anxiety in my stomach.

"Why so quiet?" she asked.

I shrugged. How could I explain that being around her husband was a problem for me, when we were supposed to just be friends? We both knew the truth was far from that, but pretending was part of the deal. "Just tired," I lied.

"Al's not here," she volunteered without me asking. "We had a bit of a spat earlier, and he jumped at a chance to go help a friend who was having car trouble."

The relief I felt was palpable. I tried not to show how happy that made me. I felt almost giddy. I knew she continued to struggle in her marriage, but details were usually sparse. My hope for a future with her remained strong.

I helped Beth bring the food out to the dining room table, which she had already set. Beth opened the bottle of wine I had brought and added it to the table along with another bottle of white. Surrounded by beautiful sisters, I sat with Jen on one side of me and Beth on the other. The conversation flowed freely and easily. This was the first time that I had an opportunity to get to know Jen's husband, Roger, and he proved to be quite entertaining.

❖

I had just walked into my apartment several hours later when my cell phone rang with Beth's ringtone. I smiled to myself. "Hello," I said. "Hello. Beth? Beth?" I could hear noises but couldn't make them out. She must have butt-dialed me, I thought. Then I heard her voice, but she wasn't talking to me. She was talking to her husband. She was talking to *him.* She had no idea I could hear her. I wondered if I should stay on the phone and listen. Would anything she said to him be reassuring to me or would it be torture? Al said something I couldn't quite make out and she answered him. They were talking about his shoes being wet. Normal stuff. Everyday stuff—reminding me that that was her life—every day—her life with him. I hung up the phone. It was too painful to listen to them spending their life together. A normal, everyday life.

What was I doing? My heart went from being light to being crushed in the blink of an eye. That's all I could expect from wanting her. It had never hit home like it did at that moment. The pain seeped around my heart and squeezed it like a fist. The blood could barely get through and pump to the rest of my body. My brain felt the loss of blood as my heart felt the loss of a dream. Let go. Let go with love. But how? How did I let go of what my heart wanted? What my heart screamed for. Yes, screamed. I struggled to keep the scream from traveling up my throat as it threatened to pour out into the world, making my heartache a reality. But it was reality. Wasn't it? She was with him. She had chosen him. She was my *friend.* Only my friend. We both knew that wasn't true. But knowing and doing something about it were two different things.

But the thing about that loss was that she was never mine to lose. That knowledge did nothing to take the sting out of it. The pain was real. It hurt, like waking up from a good dream where you're with the one you love only to discover that she wasn't in your arms after all. When the reality of the morning wakes you from that dream, you know you have to let it go. That was the point I was at. I needed to figure out how to let it go. I didn't know if I could do that and still keep her in my life. Seeing her, talking to her on the phone, even texting with her only made me want her more.

The solution was one I didn't want to face. I had to tell Beth I needed time away from her to think, to heal. It was the hardest thing I ever had to do.

❖

I walked through life in the weeks that followed without seeing anything around me. Why even bother looking? The world had lost its color and even the black and white that remained was more like a muted gray. It lacked contrast. It lacked meaning. I avoided everyone, everything. Annie was back from Denver and knew something was wrong but didn't know what. No one knew what I was going through. I was grieving in silence. My loss was mine alone. Telling myself that it was for the best didn't make the pain any less. Telling myself that the Universe was protecting me from future hurt didn't stop the current pain.

I worked on projects. I smiled at clients. I struggled to keep the sadness that filled my heart from reaching my eyes and pouring out into the world. I think for the most part it worked. If anyone saw my pain they didn't let on. I wanted to scream at them. LOOK AT ME! LOOK AT WHAT I'M GOING THROUGH! SEE ME! But no one did. I was alone in my suffering.

I lay in bed one night and looked at the empty side of the bed. The side Beth could have been sleeping on now if she hadn't chosen him over me. She said it wasn't a choice of that, but the fact remained that she was with him, not me. As unlikely as it sounded, I understood her choice. I didn't agree with it, but I understood it. She was married. She wanted to stay married. That was easier. That was much more accepted by her church and by the world at large. Being with me would have changed everything for her. She wasn't ready for that change, and it was likely she would never be. That was what I needed to accept. It wasn't *me* she rejected. It was a new version of *her*. She couldn't see that version. Couldn't see the possibilities of it. At the end of her life, she might not have been happy or gotten what she wanted, but damn, at least no one would have thought she was gay. That I think was her biggest fear. Fear clouded her view. Fear controlled her choice. Fear ruled the world.

Fear made her want it to work with him and she needed to give it another chance. She found happiness with him once. She believed she could find it again. A part of me hoped she was right. Hoped she would be happy with him again. Another part of me wanted her to leave him, even if she didn't come to me. He didn't deserve her. She deserved someone who cherished her. Someone who would never cheat on her. He had failed on both fronts. He would hurt her again. I knew it as surely as I knew the sun would rise each morning and set each night. I longed to protect her from that hurt. I longed to hold her, to kiss her, to make love to her. My eyes teared up with the very thought of it. The thought of what I almost had. The thought of what I had lost. And I had lost her completely. She was nowhere in my life except for my heart, and that felt like it couldn't contain the love for her without bursting. I had no way to express the feelings, so they built there, pushing at the walls until they were ready to explode. The walls that were already weak from breaking into pieces and my pathetic attempt to glue them back together.

I needed to go to sleep. The prescription from the doctor helped but not enough. Sleep. Sleep delayed the pain. But only delayed it. And only for a bit. The dreams came anyway. Dreams that could never come true. I knew I needed to let go of the dream.

I ran my hand over *her* side of the bed and thought about her just across town but a world away. She was probably lying in bed asleep or trying to sleep. I wrapped my arms around her in my mind and sent her love. Unconditional, needing nothing back, love. I hoped she felt it and for a brief moment thought of me. I pictured the pink rose quartz heart I had given her and the wooden box she kept it in tucked safely away in her nightstand. In my mind's eye, she reached over in the dark and quietly opened the drawer and removed it from the box. She clutched in her closed hand and held it close to her heart as she drifted off to sleep, thinking of me and feeling my love.

Beth

I wasn't sure what made me do it, but I reached into the drawer of my nightstand and pulled out the pink heart Jodi had given me. I rubbed my fingers over it letting the smoothness seep into my soul. The stone seemed to radiate warmth into me the same way Jodi's heart did when we were together. I closed my fingers around it and brought it to my chest. This was the only way I could have Jodi's heart next to mine. I missed that heart. I missed my friend. I missed the woman that meant so much to me. I knew the cord that connected us was still there, but she had said she needed time away from me and I gave it to her.

Al let out a snore as he rolled over onto his back beside me. I had made my choice. The only one I felt I could. I closed my eyes, and with that stone in my hand and my *choice* lying next to me in bed, I fell asleep.

Al was up and already off to work, I assumed, when I woke up the following morning. The rose quartz was still in my hand, warm from my sleep. I placed it back in its wooden box in my nightstand, safely away from the confusion and upset that was my life.

Al's toothbrush lay over the edge of his sink. Proof that he had been here and was gone. If he kissed me good-bye I didn't remember it. It was more likely he didn't. He was on his best behavior, but deep down he was who he was, and who he was was a man who didn't show much affection...at least not to me. I didn't know what kind of affection he had given to the woman he'd cheated on me with.

If I was going to make this work—and I was determined to—I needed to forgive and forget. I believed I was well on the way to forgiveness, but forgetting was another matter. It would take time. I prayed for the happiness to return to our marriage. I knew that if the marriage worked, I could be happy again. I felt so alone in the world. There was a palpable disconnect between Al and me, and Jodi's swift exit from my life left me feeling even more miserable. Between the two though, I found it was Jodi I missed the most. I was starting to wonder if I had made the biggest mistake of my life.

Jodi

What did it feel like to miss someone who I really had no right to miss? Someone who had a piece of my heart that was so big I was sure I couldn't go on living without her near. Without the piece of my heart that she held, my heart didn't seem to have the strength to beat in the rhythm it was meant to.

I sat cross-legged on the floor and set the book I'd been reading facedown, still opened to the page I was on. *How to Move On*, I read the title one more time. I needed to get on with my life. I hadn't seen Beth in a few months, and I was having a hard time letting her go. I had done each exercise in the book and was on the very last one—metaphorically cutting the cord that connected us. I did a short meditation focusing on each part of my body in turn allowing it to relax. I pictured Beth in my mind. My heart leapt, but I pushed it back into its place. I pictured a cord running between us joining us at the heart. It was made up of multiple strands, some thick, some thin, all wrapped and weaved together. It seemed unbreakable. In my mind's eye, I started with the thinner threads on the outside and pulled them apart with my hands. Soon the strands grew thicker as I got to inner portions. My hands would no longer work. I imagined a knife, a hunting knife, and hacked away at them. My arm grew tired with the effort. The cord didn't want to let loose and some of the threads held tight. I mentally switched to a handsaw and got through a few more. When I was exhausted and done, there was one single strand left. No matter what I did I couldn't get it to break. It still connected Beth and me. Maybe it was meant to last, meant to always connect us in a way that no one else could see, but we could still feel. Surely, one single thread couldn't hurt me as much as that cord did. I had no choice but to allow it to remain. I looked at the strand and sent a wave of love along it. It was the only way I had of expressing what was inside me. I tried to force all of my love for Beth through it and out of my body. I felt the ripple as the energy flowed from me to her, but only a portion of it flowed. The rest remained in my heart.

I got up and shook each leg to get the blood flowing again. I had no idea if the exercise would help. I found Beth was never far from my mind.

She'd hurt me like no one ever had before. I know she didn't mean to. How much grieving could I do over one person? The depth of my pain had surprised me—as did the depth of my love. The stomach pains that had started when Andrew joined the military had continued. But now I attributed them to the pain of missing Beth.

I felt like I had no control of the physical or emotional pain. And that pissed me off. Maybe the lesson was that control, like everything else in life, was an illusion—a promise that could never be. I dreamt of love. I dreamt of a life and connection like I'd never know before. That dream was like a candle flame that burns bright one second but flips and bends with the reality of the slightest breeze—easily extinguished with a single breath.

I needed to get my life together. Annie had asked if she could go back and stay with her father before school started. She had reconnected with old friends in Denver over the summer and felt like her life was there for a while. My small apartment probably seemed like a hole in the wall compared to her father's house.

I knew she would be better off there and I could take the time I needed to heal from Beth. I reluctantly agreed. I cried for three hours straight after I put her on the plane. My mother, Beth, and now Annie. How much more loss could I endure?

Beth

I walked into my old house and turned on the living room light. I absently picked up one of Maddie's sweaters hanging off the edge of a chair, folded it, and placed it neatly on the seat. I had to admit that for the most part Maddie was taking good care of the place.

"Hi, Mom," she said, bounding down the stairs. "Want to go out to lunch or eat here?"

I couldn't help but laugh. "I figured if you were inviting me over, you would be making us lunch."

I followed Maddie into the dining room. The table was set for two, including wine glasses and cloth napkins.

"Just kidding. I made your favorite."

"Prime rib?"

"I mean I made your second favorite. Have a seat. I'll get it." She went into the kitchen and returned with a basket of garlic bread in one hand and small pan of lasagna in the other. It brought me back to the first time I had invited Jodi over for lunch.

Maddie must have read the look on my face. "What's wrong? Something else going on with Al?" I hadn't shared the details of Al's infidelity, but she did know there were some problems in the marriage.

I shook my head. "No. He's been stepping up to the plate. It's just…" I wasn't sure how much to say. If she noticed that Jodi wasn't in my life anymore she hadn't said anything.

"Come on, Mom. You can tell me." She sat across from me. "What's going on? You haven't been yourself for months now."

I hadn't told anyone about my feelings for Jodi or how our friendship had played out. I missed Jodi terribly. I had come close to telling my sister, Jen, but feared her judgment. Maybe Maddie was the one to confide in. The secret and loss were eating me alive.

"Mom?"

"Do you remember my friend Jodi?"

"Sure. You haven't mentioned her in a while. I just assumed you had gone your separate ways."

I poured myself a glass of wine before continuing. "She has come in and out of my life. Some of it my choice, lately it's been her choice. She was—is…" I hesitated. I took a large sip of the liquid courage from my wine glass. I told Maddie the whole story.

She listened without interrupting. I wiped my tears with my napkin as the truth I had been holding in poured out of me. "Oh, Mom," she said when I had finished. "I'm so sorry."

"You don't think I'm a horrible person for loving another woman?"

"No way. I just want you to be happy. Besides, there's a difference between doing something out of love or out of obligation. You shouldn't stay with Al if it's only out of obligation."

I hadn't considered that, but she was right. That was the only reason I was trying to work things out with him. Suddenly, things came into focus. I had been fighting for something that wasn't worth fighting for. But Jodi was. Jodi was definitely worth fighting for.

"What are you going to do?"

"What can I do? Jodi needed time away from me. I'm not sure forever would be long enough for her. I know I hurt her deeply. All I want is to be with her."

"What about Al?"

"No matter how hard I try I just can't seem to gather up any feelings for him. I'm not sure I ever really had any. I think he may have been an escape from my feelings for Jodi."

Maddie cut a piece of lasagna and put it on my plate. "You need to eat something—to go with that wine."

I looked at the glass in my hand and realized I had drained it. "Maddie, I just want to be with her. What should I do?" If you had told me years ago that I would be asking my now twenty-three-old daughter for advice I would have called you crazy. Now all I wanted to hear was her opinion.

"What do you think would happen if you told her how you feel?"

I poured more wine into my glass. "I don't know. We haven't talked for months. I have no idea if she has changed her mind about me. I don't know what her feelings are."

Maddie waved her hand indicating that I should eat.

"What if I tell her and she doesn't want me?"

"Oh, but what if she does?"

A rush of adrenaline went through me at the possibility. I had made the choice to stay with Al months ago. It had been a mistake. My choice should have been Jodi. I should have gone with my heart and not my head. My heart and head finally agreed. Jodi. It was Jodi I wanted. It had been her all along. I was just too scared to face it. It was going to take courage to risk my heart. It was going to take even more courage to tell the world. I knew I could muster up the strength to do both of those things now. I just prayed I wasn't too late.

Jodi

The pain in my stomach wasn't subsiding.

"Jodi Michaels?" the nurse called. I put down the magazine I was thumbing through and followed her to the exam room.

"You've lost weight," she said when I stepped on the scale. I wasn't surprised. My appetite hadn't been very good as of late.

"That's a good thing, isn't it?"

She didn't answer. Once in the exam room, she took my vitals and recorded them on the computer without much chitchat. "The doctor will be right in." With that she was gone.

I let out a breath. I wondered if I was just wasting my time. I knew stress could do a whole of things to the body. I wasn't surprised my stomach had been so off.

About ten minutes later, there was a light knock on the door, immediately followed by my doctor entering the room. "Hello, Jodi. Not feeling too well, huh?"

"It's probably nothing. It just doesn't seem to be going away."

"Let's find out what's going on. Hop up on the exam table." She sat at the computer and reviewed the information the nurse had logged.

I filled her in about how I was feeling as she listened to my heart and lungs. She gently tugged down my lower eye lid and looked at my eye. "You look a little jaundiced. I think we need to run some tests. I want to rule out hepatitis and gall bladder problems."

"Hepatitis?" I was surprised. I expected her to say it was stress and prescribe me something to help.

"Do you smoke?"

"No. Never have."

"Do you have a history of cancer in your family?"

Hepatitis? Cancer? Should I be worried? Was it more than stress? "My mom died of pancreatic cancer a few years ago."

"Heart disease?" I knew she must have all this information in my records.

"My dad had a heart attack six months after my mother died. Do you think stress is causing heart problems?"

"Your heart sounded good. I'm going to order an EKG anyway. Let's get some blood tests and a couple of scans."

"What?" I didn't like the look on her face. Fear started to wrap around my heart.

"Don't start worrying yet. Could be something simple. I just want to start ruling things out." She typed a few more things into the computer and stood. "The nurse will be back in a few minutes with all the paperwork. Don't wait on these tests. Make an appointment for next week at the front desk before you leave."

"Okay," was all I could manage to say. None of this was what I expected. My first thought was to call my mom. But, of course, that wasn't a possibility. My second thought was to call Beth.

Beth

I felt so much better—stronger somehow—after talking to Maddie. I had told someone about my feelings for Jodi and she had been supportive. Loving. Accepting. It was time to go home and tell Al that it was over. I believed his remorse and efforts to save our marriage were sincere. But that didn't matter anymore. I didn't love him. I loved Jodi. I was determined to win her back whatever it took.

"Al," I called when I got home.

"Upstairs in my office," he called back.

"Can you come down here, please?" I set my purse on the end table and sat on the couch to wait.

"Hi, honey. What's up?" He sat next to me.

This was going to be harder than I thought. I still cared about him. I didn't like hurting people, and that included him.

"What's going on?" he said again.

I searched for the right words. I knew whatever I said was going to sound lame. He had put in a true effort to save our marriage, and here I was about to tear it apart. "This isn't working for me." Not the best start, but I truly wasn't sure how to do it any better.

"What do you mean?"

"Marriage. Our marriage. It isn't working for me."

He stood and ran a hand through his hair. "What more do you want me to do? I have done every single thing you asked."

I couldn't tell if he was getting angry or just frustrated. "I know you have. I'm just not happy."

He shook his head. "Not happy? Not happy?" He stared at me in disbelief. "Look, honey…" He sat back down and took my hands. "Tell me what you want. I'll do it. I told you I've changed. I did that for you."

I pulled my hands away from him. "I want a divorce."

"You've got to be kidding me." I could tell that was his anger coming through. "What the hell? I did everything you asked. I've given you everything you wanted. And you are telling me it's not enough?"

I considered using the classic line, *It's not you, it's me*. But I didn't think that would help. There was no way I was going to tell him about my feelings for Jodi or the real reason I was leaving.

"I'm sor—" I started.

"Oh, you're sorry. You're sorry." Yes, he was angry and it was escalating. I stood up and he grabbed my hand. "Don't. Sit down. We need to talk about this."

I yanked my hand out of his. There wasn't anything else to talk about. I wasn't happy. I wasn't staying. End of conversation.

"Please," he said. "Please talk to me. Don't do this." His anger turned to pleading. That felt far worse. I was torn between going upstairs and packing a bag or sitting back down. I chose to sit.

"I'm not going to change my mind."

"I am so confused right now. I thought things were going good. I love you. I don't want to lose you. I'm asking you not to do this, please." He had definitely crossed over to begging. For a split second, I considered giving in. But I remembered why I was leaving him. Jodi. There was no one else in the world for me. Jodi. I stood up again, resolved to do what I had to.

"I'm moving my stuff into the guest room. I'll figure out where I'm going to go tomorrow. I *am* sorry." With that, I grabbed my purse and went up the stairs without looking back at him. I ignored him when he called my name again. I wasn't so much leaving someone as going toward someone. Something. Love.

Jodi

I hadn't told anyone about the tests the doctor had ordered. I sat alone in the exam room waiting for the doctor to come in with my results. I vacillated between being nervous and telling myself not to worry.

To my surprise, I had gotten a text from Beth that morning asking me to meet. I wanted to get this out of the way before answering her. If this was serious, I knew I would need her. Need to let her know. Need to have her support. If it wasn't, there was no sense having her worry. Even though she had chosen her husband I knew she still loved me, or at the very least still cared about me.

A light knock on the door and my doctor walked in, papers in hand. I couldn't quite read the look on her face. "How are you feeling?" she asked.

"Anxious. What's the verdict here? Did you find out what's wrong with me?"

"I did." She paused and I sensed it wasn't going to be good news. "You have pancreatic cancer."

What? No. No. No. What? My brain wasn't firing correctly. People die from that. My mother died from that. That wasn't stress. That wasn't even hepatitis. That was cancer. That was a very bad cancer. I was going to die.

"I know that's hard to hear. I think we've caught it early. There are treatments. It's not something we would have normally tested for given your age. But because of your mother I added it to our tests."

It didn't make sense. I was going to die. Wait. What? Treatments? Treatments where all my hair would fall out and I would die anyway? Die without my hair. Nothing was making sense.

"Jodi? I know this is a lot to take in. Do you have any questions for me?"

"No." No questions. Nothing more to say. I was going to die with no hair.

"I've set up a referral for an oncologist. Do you have a certain doctor or place you would like to go to?"

"No. I have no idea." I needed my mother. But my mother wasn't here. She had died. Died of cancer. I had cancer now. I would be dying soon. My thoughts turned to my kids. Annie with her father in Denver. She would be living with him permanently now. Andrew was stationed in Okinawa, Japan. They would be left without a mother. I knew how much that hurt. I didn't want my kids to hurt that way. Beth. I needed to tell Beth.

I had a million thoughts, yet my mind felt blank. Empty. Numb.

I had cancer.

Beth

I waited a week after I left Al and moved back into my own house with Maddie before I contacted Jodi. I wanted to call but was afraid I would cry when I talked to her. I sent a text, like a coward. I simply said I wanted to see her. She waited a whole day before she answered. I was in a state of near panic the whole time. Her text back was just as simple.

Can you meet me at my apartment tomorrow at noon?

I answered immediately. *Of course.*

She didn't text back after that. I had no idea what to expect. The butterflies that took up residence in my stomach kept me from sleeping that night. The next morning, they kept me from eating breakfast. A cup of coffee and a whole lot of pacing were the only things that kept them even a little bit under control.

I pulled into the parking lot of Jodi's building several minutes early and sat in my car. Waiting. Watching the minutes tick by. At exactly eleven fifty-nine, I climbed the steps to her apartment, went down the hallway, and knocked on the door.

She greeted me with a tight hug. When she released me and stepped back, she was still beautiful, but her eyes looked swollen and red. I could tell she'd been crying. She'd lost weight since I had last seen her. She looked drawn and I wondered if that was due to me and the hurt I had caused. The hurt I had hoped to make up for even if it took me the rest of my life. Because that's what I wanted to give her—the rest of my life. Fully. Completely.

"There's something I wanted to talk to you about," I said, still unsure of the reaction I would get.

"Me too. But we need to sit down first." She took my hand and led me to the couch. But she started talking before I had a chance to sit down. "I…um." She started. "I haven't been feeling too good lately."

I nodded. I could tell.

"I have cancer. I'm dying."

"What?" I sank down on the couch. All the air left my lungs and I struggled for breath. This couldn't be real. It wasn't real. It wasn't.

"Are you all right?" Jodi asked.

No. I wasn't all right. My world had just come crashing down on me. I brought my eyes up to hers. Concern radiated out to me. To *me*. Her concern was for me. That made no sense. None of this made sense.

She sat by my side and I reached out to stroke her hair. Despite the news she had just shared with me, a tingle ran down my arm at the contact. I rested my forehead against hers. Tears leaked out of my closed eyes. "Oh my God," I whispered. It was all I could manage to say.

I felt her arms go around me and pull me in tighter. For a brief moment, the horrible truth left my mind and I was filled with the closeness of her. She felt so alive in my arms. How could she be dying?

"What? How?" I managed to say after several long minutes.

"Pancreatic cancer. The doctor said they caught it early, but I know the statistics for this aren't good. I have a very bad feeling about it."

"So, no one actually told you you were actually dying? What did the doctor say exactly?"

She filled me in on the details. I was still scared, but there was hope.

"I left Al," I blurted out.

"Why?" she asked.

"To be with you. I made a terrible mistake staying with him and losing you."

Her anger surprised me. She stood and turned toward me. "*Now* you leave him? You need to go back."

I fought back the tears. She didn't want me anymore. "No. You don't understand. I don't want him. I want you. I was hoping you felt the same."

She turned her back to me. "It doesn't matter what I feel anymore. Don't you get it? I'm not going to be around."

I stood up and wrapped my arms around her. "Don't say that."

She shook me off. "I have nothing left to offer you."

Now I was the one getting angry. She wasn't going to push me away. Not this time. "I'm not asking you to give me anything. I'm asking you to let me give to you."

"No." Was her simple answer.

I pulled her back down to the couch with me. "I'm not letting you go like this."

"You won't have a choice. I'm not going to push you out of my life, but don't you understand that I don't have much life left? I'm not trying to be overly dramatic here, Beth."

We would check out every option and treatment there was. She wouldn't die. She couldn't. I would make sure we turned over every stone. I wouldn't give up. And I wouldn't let her either.

"Beth, we can't be together. We had our chance and we didn't take it. Now it's too late."

I needed to figure out the right words to say to her, to make her understand that I was there for her. For whatever she needed. For however long she had. I tried again to explain, but my words fell on deaf ears. She had made up her mind, and apparently, I wasn't going to be able to change it.

"When is your next doctor's appointment?" If she refused to be my partner at least I could be her friend.

"Tuesday with the oncologist."

"I'm going with you."

"Beth—"

"I'm going with you. I'll pick you up. Tell me what time."

She didn't answer.

"Tell me."

"I have to be there at ten a.m."

"I'll be here at nine. Does that give us enough time?"

"Beth, you don't have to—"

"Does that give us enough time?" I asked again, this time much more firmly.

"Yes."

"When's the last time you ate?" I got up and went to the refrigerator. "Huh? Last time?"

"I think it was yesterday."

She didn't have much in the way of food. I pulled out a package of lunch meat, sniffed it, and decided it was still good. I grabbed a jar of mustard and the bread from the counter and proceeded to make us both a sandwich. I didn't have much of an appetite with everything that had just happened, but figured I had a better chance of getting Jodi to eat if I ate with her.

I didn't know how we were going to get through this, but I refused to give up. Whether she ever decided to be with me didn't matter in that moment. Getting her back to health was the only thing that did. I knew next to nothing about pancreatic cancer, but I was determined to find out.

JODI

There was no way I was going to let Beth throw her life away on someone who was dying. I had nothing left to give—to anyone.

My mind was still numb from the devastating news. Bits and pieces of what I needed to do filtered through. Who did I need to tell? Should I let my kids know now or wait till this horrid disease had progressed more? I wanted to keep them away from my pain as long as possible. What about my business? I had orders for three signs I needed to work on. Should I bother? Should I close my business completely? Would my health insurance cover my end of life expenses or would I leave me kids with medical bills? My head was swirling, and I couldn't seem to get it to stop.

Too many questions and no real answers. Sleeping had become impossible. The exhaustion made reasonable thinking even more difficult.

As she said she would, Beth was at my door Tuesday morning at nine o'clock to take me to my appointment. We pulled up in front of the hospital and she let the valet service park the car. I handed her the paperwork my doctor had given me and let her lead the way to the oncology department and check me in.

It seemed to take forever before my name was called and we were led to a room in the back. We were left there alone for another fifteen minutes. Beth tried to make small talk, but my brain refused to engage enough to give her much more than one- or two-word answers.

A tall man with a white goatee that was a shade darker than his white coat entered the room. "Miss Michaels?"

I nodded.

"I'm Dr. Daniels." He extended a hand. I absently shook it.

He turned to Beth. "Hello."

She introduced herself.

"Sister? Friend?" the doctor asked her.

She hesitated only a moment. "Friend. But more than that. Jodi is very important to me."

"Of course." He turned to me. "I have your test results here. I understand your mother died of pancreatic cancer. I'm sure you're scared. What she had was stage four, as I'm sure you know. We caught yours much sooner. So the prognosis can be much better."

"Can be?" He didn't say it was. Only that it *could* be.

"Yes," he continued. "You have stage one. That means that right now it's confined to the pancreas itself. It hasn't spread. That's a good thing. Treatment options include surgery, radiation, chemo…" He continued, but it was too much for me to take in. I glanced at Beth. She seemed to be listening intently. I hoped she was absorbing the information better than I was.

"…and of course, there are several trials you can apply for."

"What are the trials?" Beth asked. "Do you know anything about their success rates?"

He answered that and several other questions she asked about surgery and various treatments.

I didn't see the reason for all the questions. I was going to die. My mother died. I would be next. My children would be left without a mother.

"Do you have any questions?" The doctor, I couldn't remember his name, addressed me.

I shook my head.

"I'm sure this is a lot to absorb. We don't want to wait too long before starting treatment, but you can take a few days to think about, talk it over with your friend here." He nodded toward Beth. "I have a packet here"—he handed a folder to Beth—"with all the information I went over. Look through it and see what you think. I suggest you don't use the internet for research. There is a lot of misinformation out there. I would be happy to answer any questions you have. My number is on the first page. Just leave a message with my service and I'll get back to you."

Beth thumbed through the papers in the folder. "Are the current trials in here?"

"They are. You can stop at the desk and make another appointment. I'd like to see you back within a few days so we can discuss a plan."

"I want you to come live with me," Beth said on the ride home.

"No."

"Why not?"

I just shrugged. There was no way I was going to become a burden to anyone. Especially Beth. I had been with my mother at the end. I knew what that was like. It was horrendous watching someone die, but the daily cleaning, feeding, and care was too much to ask of someone.

"Did you hear anything that doctor said?"

I nodded.

Her voice went up in volume. It stopped just short of yelling. "What the hell is wrong with you?"

I shrugged again.

"Jodi, you've got to fight this," she said. I could hear the compassion in her voice. "I want to be with you through this. I want to be with you, period."

"I've already said that's not going to happen." I didn't look at her. I didn't want to see the expression on her face. I didn't want her pity—or her anger. The time had passed that we could ever be together.

BETH

Jodi was confusing and frustrating the hell out of me. I didn't understand why she wasn't willing to fight for her life. I had been afraid of the world seeing me loving another woman. Now I was afraid I would lose that woman forever.

I dropped her off at her apartment. She didn't invite me in and I didn't push. I held off the tears until she closed the door to the apartment building behind her. I slammed my fists against the steering wheel until my hands went numb.

I roughly wiped the tears from my cheeks and drove to my sister's house.

"You look like you've been crying. What's going on? Is it Al again?" She hadn't bothered to say hello. She gave me a hug. "Come on, let's go out back. I'll get us iced tea."

I followed her to the kitchen, where she poured two glasses of iced tea, and out the back door to the deck. I had always envied Jen's backyard. She, like my mother, was a master at gardening. Flowers in an array of colors lined up along the edge of the house and stood at attention in a circle surrounded by a stone border in the center of the yard.

I pulled out a chair and sat at the glass patio table. Jen set a glass of iced tea in front of me and sat on the opposite side of the table.

A few tears leaked from my eyes. Without a word, Jen went back into the house and brought out a stack of napkins. I dabbed at my eyes.

"Speak," Jen said.

"I left Al," I started.

"Oh, honey, that must have been so hard. I'm so sorry."

I let out a laugh. The irony of it all hit me. "That was the easy part."

"And what is the hard part?"

"Do you remember Jodi?"

"Of course."

I took a swallow of the tea. I needed a moment to compose myself. "She's sick. Cancer."

Jen leaned forward. "Oh my God, Beth. I'm so sorry." She reached her hand across the table and placed it over mine. "I know you were close."

"Close is an understatement." It was time for the truth to be told. I had spent too much time running from it—running from myself.

"What does that mean?"

I looked my sister straight in the eye. I took a deep breath, then looked away. A few more tears ran down my cheeks. Not as easy as I thought it would be. "I'm…" I turned back to face Jen. "I'm in love with her. I have been for a long time."

I didn't know Jen's eyes could open that wide. It took her a moment to compose herself. "That's not something…" She shook her head. "I'm just surprised…" She cleared her throat and started again. "Okay. Does she feel the same way about you?"

"She did. I don't know anymore. She seems to have given up on life. On everything. She just recently found out about the cancer and she's not handling it well."

"What can I do to help?"

I wasn't sure what to expect from my sister, but her kindness surprised me. "Nothing. Just…I don't know. I just needed someone to talk to. I don't know what to do to help her. I can't let her die. I just can't."

"Of course not." She handed me another napkin and I realized I had twisted the first one into a wet wad. "Does this mean you're gay?"

"I don't know what it means." That was the truth. "Do we have to label it?"

"Have you been attracted to any other women in your life?" I guess the questions were to be expected. I never gave any indication that this was even possible.

"Nope."

"Maybe you're pansexual."

"I don't even know what that means."

"It's a sexual or romantic attraction toward someone regardless of their gender. You fall in love with their heart."

"That sounds like it fits."

"Have you told anyone else this?"

"I told Maddie about my feelings and why I left Al. She was very supportive. I haven't told her about the cancer yet." I wanted to know more about the treatment options and what decisions Jodi would make before telling her.

"You left Al because of Jodi?"

"I did. But when I told Jodi that, she said no. She said she didn't have anything to offer."

"How did you feel about that?"

"Freaking heartbroken. But the cancer and the fear of losing her...of her dying..." I closed my eyes. The possibility of her dying was more than I could bear. I cleared my throat. "Her cancer kind of overshadowed the fact that she had just rejected me. I'm still going to fight for her. Fight to be with her and help her fight for her life."

"And how are you going to do that if she won't let you in?"

"I have no idea. But I'm going to give it everything I've got."

Jodi

It was hard to admit it to myself, but I was pretty pissed at Beth. Why couldn't she have made the decision to leave Al and be with me before I got sick? Don't get me wrong, I appreciated her help now. I appreciated that she brought me to the doctors the day before. But it almost seemed like too little too late. She broke my heart when she chose Al over me. Chose a straight marriage that wasn't working because it was easier for her. All I wanted was her back. Now that I had that chance I knew it wouldn't work. I wasn't going to be around much longer. No one said that to me, but that's what I felt.

Did I still love her? Absolutely. But the feeling of love felt watered down, drowned out by this killer disease.

I picked up the folder the doctor had given me and thumbed through it. I looked through a few pages. It was all so overwhelming. I sent the folder flying across the room. It hit the wall and papers scattered everywhere. This wasn't fair. What the fuck kind of cruel sense of humor did the Universe have? At this moment, I could have had it all. I could have had Beth, my children, my business. But I was going to lose everything.

"What the fuck?" I screamed.

My door opened and Beth walked in. "That's a good question." She stepped over the papers littering the floor. "I was going to ask you how you're doing. But it doesn't look like you're doing too good."

She sat on the couch next to me and took my hands. "Look at me," she said.

It took several long seconds for me to comply. Two weeks ago, I would have given almost anything to look into those beautiful eyes. Why was it so hard now?

She leaned her forehead against mine for a minute.

"I'm here for you. Whether you want me here or not. So stop acting like an ass. Can you do that for me?"

"I can't believe you would say that to a sick person," I said but couldn't help but smile.

"I can say that to the person I love."

I wasn't sure I wanted to hear her say that. I didn't want her to stop loving me, but it hurt to know her love would be left hanging after I died.

"You have some decisions to make. I see you at least picked up the folder." She waved her hand toward the papers littering the floor. "Did you actually look at them?"

"A few."

"Did you make any decisions?"

I shook my head. I had barely taken in what was on the pages.

"Jodi. You have to do this. I'll help you any way I can. But you're the one who has to make the final decisions here."

She rubbed my back. Her hand was soft and warm, and at first, I resented the fact that it was a comfort to me. Slowly, I let the love she felt seep through her fingers and into me. I let out an audible sigh.

"That's better," she said. "Talk to me. I know you're scared. I'm scared too. What's going through your head?"

Her words struck a chord with me. I wasn't willing to give her my heart, but I was willing to let her in on some truths. "I watched my mother die from this same disease. Literally watched her die a little each day."

"You told me what she died of, but you didn't share any of the details with me. Do you think you can tell me about it now?"

I closed my eyes as the images of her in her last days floated through my mind. "The kids and I went to Denver as soon as she was diagnosed. Stage four pancreatic cancer. For the most part, she was herself. She kept her sense of humor, her faith in God, her love for her family." I took a deep breath before continuing. It felt both good and frightening to be sharing it with Beth. She would soon know the truth about the horrors of this disease. "We stayed about a week but had to get back because the kids had school."

I remembered every detail as if it had just happened. My mother was pale and thin. It was almost frightening to look at her. She lasted almost four months to the day from diagnosis to death. "I returned without the kids and spent the last two weeks of her life with her. She and my dad had decided to do home hospice. Which actually meant we did the majority of caring for her."

Beth grabbed some tissues from the box on the end table by the couch and handed them to me. Tears rolled down my cheeks and I swiped at them. I had sobbed for weeks after my mother's death. I was surprised I had more tears to shed.

"Anyway, death isn't pretty. It's not like you see in the movies. I watched my mother waste away as the cancer invaded her other organs and eventually her bones. I wasn't sure at times if she was clinging to life or reaching for the release that only death can bring. It was like she could graze it with her fingertips only to find it was still beyond her grasp. At the end, she was in a morphine haze. It was the only thing that could control her pain."

"Jodi, I'm so sorry you had to go through that."

"The hardest part was watching my dad go through it. She was the love of his life and he lost her." I dabbed at my eyes with a tissue. "He was a trooper though. Kept her clean and hand-fed her broth and such when she got too weak to eat. I took the night shift and slept in a chair by her bed every night for two weeks. The one night I decided to sleep in an actual bed in the guest room is the night she died."

"You're not blaming yourself in any way are you?"

I let out a puff of air. I knew when I decided not to spend the night in that room I had to be prepared for that to happen. I'd heard enough stories about people holding on until a loved one left the vicinity. I actually wondered if I had prolonged my mother's suffering by staying so close by. "No. I'm not. But the whole thing was devastating to watch."

It is an interesting and horrific thing to watch the life leak out of a person. Especially a person your soul was wrapped around. The tangle of lines that connected us was coming unjumbled as my mother slipped into her own destiny without us.

"I can only imagine. Sometimes I think I was lucky losing my father suddenly in a car accident so I didn't have to see him suffer."

That was the exact reason I wouldn't be letting Beth too deeply back into my life. I couldn't let her see me waste away and die in front of her.

"So…" she said, getting to her feet. "Let's go over these papers and at least educate ourselves on the options." She began to pick the papers up from the floor and put them back in some kind of order.

Okay, I would let her help me with this. But I would watch carefully for the right time to let her go and send her out of my life. It would hurt her, I knew. But it wouldn't hurt her nearly as much as watching me die.

Beth

I glanced over at Jodi as I retrieved the scattered papers. Her being with Claire had kept us apart. Me marrying Al had done the same thing, as well as an unhealthy dose of fear on my part. I'd be damned if I'd let her illness do the same thing now.

She was in shock. I knew that. Having the same disease that killed your mother had to be devastating. I was determined to get her through this.

With the stack of papers in somewhat order, I sat next to Jodi. We went through each page one by one. We discussed the options and I made sure Jodi understood everything. She had a lot of knowledge about the cancer itself, but not the treatments. Her mother's cancer was so far advanced when it was discovered that treatments weren't really an option.

"Do you think you should get a second opinion?" I asked her.

"No. Maybe. What do you think?"

"I think it's a good idea."

"I don't know."

I shook my head. "Yes, no, I don't know."

"Are you making fun of me?"

I wrapped my arms around her. I wasn't sure if she was going to let me, but she did. "Oh, honey, no. I'm just trying to help." She was warm in my arms. I longed to kiss her, but I settled for holding her tight.

I held on as long as she would allow it. After a couple of minutes, she shook me off. "I don't want chemo," she said.

"What *do* you want?"

"I don't think a second opinion is necessary. The doctor said the tumor is only in the pancreases. He said surgery would be necessary, even though it's a pretty complicated procedure. I'm not sure after that."

"Actually, you need to figure out what to do first." I knew she was in a fog when we talked to the oncologist. But there were key things she seemed to have missed. I explained the treatments that he recommended to start with to make surgery more successful. Chemo and radiation were usually the first steps. We would have to check out the trials to see if there was an alternative.

She seemed to take it all in. "I definitely want to learn more about the trials."

I thumbed through the papers on my lap and pulled out the sheets I was searching for. "There are phone numbers for the different trials to get more information. We would have to see what you qualify for. Not all of them are for stage one. Have you told your kids, yet?"

She shook her head. "I haven't told anyone but you."

I was touched that she trusted me with the truth but knew she needed to let her family know. "When do you plan on telling them?"

"I don't want them to worry. I'm going to wait until I decide on a definite treatment option and everything is in place."

"You aren't going to save them from worrying. They love you. Of course, they are going to worry." I should know. I was in love with her and I was very worried. But I refused to let her see that. I vowed to show her nothing but hope and support—and whatever amount of love she would accept.

JODI

Chemo, radiation, drugs, surgery, probably more drugs. That was the life I was expecting to have before I died—leaving my children without a mother—like mine had left me.

Beth was helping me every step of the way, and I really appreciated it. But I was very aware that I needed to keep my emotional distance and make sure she kept hers. Of course, that was really hard to gauge. She always seemed to be touching me—hugs, a hand on my back, a kiss on the cheek. I didn't make her stop, but I was always careful not to let it go past that.

I stared at the phone in my hand. I had already called the base Andrew was stationed at to get a message to him. He was out on maneuvers and they weren't allowed to have their cell phones with them. I'm sure he would call when he had a chance. Not the best place to be when you find out your mother is sick.

I opened my contacts on my phone and pressed my ex-husband's name. My heart thumped heavy in my chest as I waited for him to answer.

"Hello?"

"Sammy?"

"Hi, Jodi, are you calling for Annie?"

"Um, no. I need to talk to you first." I drummed my fingers on the table. "She isn't within earshot, is she?"

"No. She's out back. What's up. You okay?"

"That's what I'm calling about. I…um…I wasn't feeling well and went to the doctor." I knew I was dragging this out more than it had to be, but I just couldn't seem to string a sentence together.

"Okay," he said tentatively.

"Turns out I have pancreatic cancer."

Silence.

"Sam?"

"Yeah. I'm here. I'm just at a loss for words. I mean, how bad?"

"Stage one."

"Okay, well… Wow. But one is the best possible, right?" He didn't seem to be too successful with talking at the moment either.

"I guess if you're gonna get a life-threatening cancer, yeah, stage one is the best."

"What did the doctors say? How serious is this?"

I shook my head. Pretty fucking serious. "Very."

"What do you want me to do? Do you need me to come there? Bring Annie?"

"No," I said a little more sternly than I had intended to. "I mean, at some point yes. I'll need to see Annie, but not yet. I'm not sure when. I don't want her here at the end. I don't want her seeing me like that."

"The end?"

My turn to be silent.

"Jodi, it's that bad? That's what they told you?"

"They didn't have to tell me. It's what killed my mother. I know how bad this can be."

"So, you don't really know." His statement pissed me off. My first instinct was to argue, but I knew that would be counterproductive. I chose to ignore it.

"Do you think we should tell Annie? Or wait?"

Beth thought she should know. My thought was the earlier she found out, the longer she would be scared and sad. I thought one more opinion was in order.

"When do your treatments start?"

"A week from yesterday. I'm starting a clinical trial to try to shrink the tumor." I explained that if that went well, we went to radiation, followed by surgery.

"I think we should wait to see how you respond to treatment. No need to worry her. You will probably come out of this fine. Let's wait a little while."

"My only concern is that I'll look like hell when she does see me. I don't want her to have that lasting image." I still saw my mother's withered body from her last days on this earth when I closed my eyes.

"You could never look like hell," he said. I know he was trying to lighten the mood, but his attempt was in vain.

I didn't answer.

"Tell me what you want to do."

"Maybe you're right. We should wait. Let's see what happens with round one. Then we can decide on the timing." I know Beth would be disappointed with my decision. But that's what it ultimately was—my decision.

"Sounds like a plan. Do you want me to call her in so you can talk to her?"

"Yeah." I cleared my throat.

"Hi, Mom," my daughter said a minute later. I could hear the excitement in her voice. She was no longer my little girl. She was a full-fledged teenager, with her whole life ahead of her. Tears sprung to my eyes at the thought of all I would miss.

"Hey, baby." I worked to keep my voice steady. "How are you doing?"

"Good. Dad said I could get a puppy." It had broken her heart when Tess died last year. I just hadn't had the time or energy for housebreaking and all the training that went into a new puppy. The truth was my heart hadn't been ready to let a new little creature into it.

"That's great. How does Barbara feel about it?" Sam had met and married Barbara a little over a year after we divorced. I'd met her on several occasions and always found her warm and pleasant. I could have easily been very insecure around her. She seemed to have it all, charm, intelligence, and true beauty. And now she had my ex-husband and daughter. Annie adored her and she treated Annie like she was her own. I was good with that. I figured the more people who loved my kids, the better off my kids would be. At times, okay, most of the time, I was jealous of the time she got to spend with Annie. But I was grateful for her presence in my daughter's life.

My intention with letting Annie go back to Denver after summer break was just to give myself time to get my life, post Claire, together so I could bring her home. I worked overtime on my business, drumming up new clients and getting jobs done in a very timely manner. I had been setting money aside for a down payment on a house. Now I would have to use that money to live on—until I wasn't alive anymore. I put my business on hold for the time being but had a call in to a broker who specialized in selling established businesses. I had used a similar service to sell my business when we left Denver. So far, he didn't have any hits.

"She said I had to be responsible for him. She got me a book on dog training. We're going tomorrow to look at a rescue place."

"That's great, honey. I'm so glad."

She went on to fill me in on her life in Denver, her school, and friends. I cried for a half hour after we hung up. How was I ever going to do this?

Beth

"How are you doing, honey?" my mom asked. "How's it going living with Maddie again?"

I cut several more slices of cheese and lined them up on the plate next to the neatly laid out crackers. "So far so good. I've been spending a lot of time with Jodi lately, helping her with all the medical stuff. I'm not home much."

"My prayer group has been praying for her since you told me about her cancer."

That word still felt like a knife to my heart. "I appreciate it, Mom." I brought the plate of cheese and crackers and added it to the other plates on the dining room table.

We had hoped the rain would let up long enough to use the grill on the back deck for the hamburgers. Roger, Jen's husband, usually did the grilling when we had a family get-together, but it was his birthday we were celebrating, so I didn't want to put that burden on him.

"Jodi is so lucky to have you helping her." My mother took the plastic cover off the top of the container and placed a four and a two candle on the top of the cake.

I toyed with the idea of telling her my feelings for Jodi but decided against it. If it didn't go well I didn't want any tension to ruin the day for Roger and Jen. She knew Jodi was gay, Maddie had mentioned it casually once, not thinking it was a big deal. It wasn't a big deal. I didn't want it to be a big deal. But my mom had been surprised that I would have a friend "like that."

"Like what?" I had asked her.

"You know. A homosexual."

"Mom, she's a regular person. And one of the best people I know."

Up until the time I got married to Al, Jodi had been in my life a lot. My mom had several opportunities to spend time with her and had grown to like her and care about her. If it made any difference that Jodi was gay, she never mentioned it again.

"I'm here." Maddie came in carrying a bag of potato chips. "Where do you want these?" she asked my mother.

"There's a bowl on the dining room table just waiting for them."

"Hi, Mom." She gave me a kiss on the cheek as she passed. "How's Jodi doing?" I appreciated the fact that she cared. "I thought she might come today."

"I asked her. She wasn't up for it." I filled her in on the plans for treatment.

I wished Jodi was there with us. I knew she wasn't up for celebrating and didn't want to bring the party down. *Down* was the word to describe Jodi lately. She was so depressed and sure she was going to die. I had inquired about an antidepressant, but it wasn't advised with the medicine in the clinical trial she was starting in a couple of days.

I had spent the morning in church, as I had the past several mornings, praying for her. For her peace, for her health, and selfishly, for her to let me in.

I had offered again to have her move in with me. She used Maddie as an excuse not to. Granted, my house was small, but we would have managed. Maddie was looking for her own apartment anyway. "It will make it easier for you to convince Jodi," she'd said. "Besides, this place is yours. You should have it back."

I was grateful for her support, in both the situation with Jodi and the situation with Al. He took to calling on a regular basis to try to get me to change my mind. He vacillated from being sickly sweet, to begging, to getting angry when I wouldn't change my mind. I stopped answering his calls.

The paperwork was in the hands of my lawyer. She knew what was going on with Jodi, and I asked her to take care of everything with minimal involvement from me. I wasn't asking Al for anything other than what I came into the marriage with. Demanding alimony would have been futile. I discovered shortly after I found out about his affair that the money he had lavished on me and the wedding—as well as his fucking mistress—was his mother's and subsequently his inheritance. And there wasn't much left.

"How's my favorite sister-in-law?" Roger asked when he and Jen arrived a little while later.

"I'm going to tell your brother's wife you said that," Jen piped in.

"Feel free," he answered her. "I'll just deny it." He gave her a love pat on the butt.

"Was that a free feel?" she teased him.

I envied their relationship. It was the stuff they wrote about in romance novels. That's what I wanted with Jodi—if she would just give it a chance. But I wasn't going to push. She had other things on her mind than my romantic notions. But that didn't stop me from having them.

Jodi

B eth took my hand as we sat in the waiting room. It was warm and comforting. I was sure mine must have been ice-cold. "Nervous?"

"Little bit," I replied. It was all I could do to keep from passing out. I forced myself to keep my breath steady so I wouldn't hyperventilate.

"Just a little bit? I guess that's good for your first procedure."

"If you believe that, I have some swampland in Florida I'm looking to sell."

"I could tell by your trembling hand that you were lying."

The room painted a calming yellow shade had twenty or so chairs lining the walls and about ten more in the center of the room. Only a dozen were occupied. Almost everyone had their eyes locked on their smartphones. A few watched the silent television hanging on the wall, words from closed captioning crawled across the bottom of the screen.

I stood up when I heard my name called, still holding on to Beth's hand.

"Can I come?" Beth asked.

"I'll come back to get you when she is all set up with a gown and IV," the nurse said.

"You got this," Beth said. She squeezed my hand. I was reluctant to let go. "I'll see you soon."

I nodded and silently followed the nurse. Her scrub suit boasted the characters from Rug Rats. It brought me back to when my kids were babies and transfixed on the TV and that cartoon.

My kids. I missed them terribly. I still hadn't told Annie what was going on, but had a hard time keeping my composure when I filled

Andrew in over the phone. He had offered to request emergency leave to come home. I asked him to hold off on that. I needed to stay focused on getting through this procedure. I didn't want to have to worry about him worrying about me.

I was led to a small room made up of one real wall in the back and three curtains that were pulled closed to make up the other three walls. A hospital gown was lying over the bed and I was instructed to remove all my clothes and change into the gown—ties in the front. I was given a large purple plastic bag with a drawstring for my clothes and a smaller one for my shoes.

I was changed and in bed with an uncomfortable IV in my arm when Beth was led into the makeshift room.

"That color looks good on you," she said. "Pale green is definitely your color."

"It kind of matches the color of your face," I answered. "You don't look so good. I think you're more nervous than I am if that's even possible."

"It is." She pulled a chair close to the bed. I hoped she would take my hand again and she didn't disappoint.

The nurse fiddled with the regulator thing on the IV tubing. "The doctor will be here in a few minutes," she said. "Do you need anything?"

"A hamburger would be nice."

She laughed. "Afraid not."

"I'll get you a hamburger once this is over and you're up to it," Beth said. She ran a finger over the back of my hand she was holding. It sent a shiver through me. I made sure she didn't see how it affected me.

"The hell with that. I want steak and lobster after this." I shook my head. "So far this isn't nearly as fun as I thought it would be."

"No, huh? Okay. Steak and lobster, it is. I promise."

Dr. Daniels pulled the curtain back and stuck his head in. "How we doing?" he asked before coming all the way in. "You ready for this?"

"Ready as I'll ever be," I answered. "Too late to run out now anyway. This gown doesn't cover up enough to escape in."

"That's the plan." He pulled a small stool up to the side of the bed and sat down. "Just to remind you, we're going to be doing targeted therapy. You chose to forgo traditional chemotherapy. We are going into the abdomen with a small cut…" He gently pulled the sheet down and opened up part of my gown, exposing my stomach. "Right here."

He pulled a black Sharpie from his coat pocket and made an X where the cut would be and signed his name above it. "We carefully snake a catheter to your pancreas and implant the medicated disc to the area above the tumor. We remove the catheter and glue the small incision." He paused, giving us a chance to absorb the information. He had explained this along with the doctor who was running the study already, but I appreciated the fact that he was going over it again. It was a lot to take in.

"The disc not only slowly releases a localize chemo med, it should also stop the tumor from invading the liver. The disc is biodegradable. It will dissolve on its own after all the medicine is released. Any questions so far?"

I shook my head. He looked over at Beth and she did the same.

"The chances of side effects are fairly low, but there have been some cases in the study ranging from mild to more severe. None have been life threatening. But some have been very unpleasant for the patient."

Beth gave my hand a squeeze. I was so glad for her support. I don't think I could have gone through this on my own.

The doctor continued. "We monitor you weekly, looking to see if the tumor is shrinking, which is our first goal. When we get to a more manageable size, we add radiation to the regiment. Final step is surgery. Best-case scenario is removal with clean margins."

"And if the margins aren't clean?" Beth asked. He had covered this before, but I'm sure she just wanted to make sure she understood it.

"Then we weigh our options. Full on chemo, more radiation, possibly a second surgery. Have you signed all the paperwork yet?"

As if on cue, the nurse came back into the room. "Got it right here." She held up stack of papers.

The doctor stood. "Very good. Any final questions?"

"Well, I'm not crazy about the fact that they would be *final* questions," I said. I was actually starting to feel better about the whole situation. I might not be dead in a matter of months after all. I kept a check on my optimism, though. I didn't want to get too hopeful. Beth, on the other hand, seemed to have enough hope for the both of us.

The doctor chuckled. "I guess I'm going to have to work on my bedside manner. Let me rephrase. Do you have any other questions before surgery?"

"I do not. Beth?"

She shook her head. "Nope. I think you covered everything quite nicely."

"All right then. After you sign the consent forms, you'll be given something to relax you and then you'll head to the OR where we'll get 'er done."

He took his leave and the nurse proceeded with the paperwork. When everything was signed and dated, she plunged a syringe into the port on the IV line.

"Is that going to put her to sleep?" Beth asked.

"It's going to relax her first, but she'll be asleep by the time she gets to the OR." She checked my vitals one more time. Everything was in order. My blood pressure was slightly higher than normal, but she said that wasn't unusual. "Anything else you need?" she asked, then left when I said no.

Several minutes later, my mind started to feel a little fuzzy. I wasn't sure if I liked it or not.

"How ya doing?" Beth asked.

Her eyes looked a little bigger than normal. "To be totally honest, I'm scared. So, if you're a praying woman, get down on your knees. I'm not telling you to actually pray. I just like my women on their knees." Beth burst out laughing and I joined in.

"Miss Michaels," a blurry man with a clipboard asked, interrupting us. He scanned my wristband.

I nodded.

"I'm Jason. I'm here to transport you to surgery. All set?"

I nodded again, afraid my speech might slur. I wasn't sure what they gave me, but I was tempted to ask if I could take some home.

He unlocked the wheels on the bed and wheeled me toward my destiny.

Beth

I held Jodi's hand, thankful she let me, until they wheeled her past the waiting room.

"You can wait here," Jason said to me. "Someone will come and get you once she wakes up in recovery."

I didn't want to let go of her hand, but I was confident in this surgery being her first step to total recovery. She was loopy and seemed to have trouble focusing her eyes. I kissed the back of the hand I was holding and then without thinking leaned over and kissed her on the mouth. In that moment, I didn't care who saw it. My confidence was overshadowed by fear. This was surgery, and anything could happen. If she minded the kiss she didn't show it. I did it so fast she didn't have time to object.

"I love you," I whispered close to her ear.

Her eyes closed, and I wasn't sure if she even heard me. I watched them take her down the hallway and out of sight around a corner before going back to the waiting room. I said a silent prayer as I sank down into the chair to wait.

It seemed like I sat there for hours, but in truth in was probably less than one. A nurse, not the one I had seen earlier, opened the waiting room door. "Who's here for Jodi Michaels?"

I stood.

"I just wanted to let you know she's in recovery. She's doing fine. Still asleep. I'll come and get you when she wakes up."

Oh my God. She was okay. "Thank you so much."

She nodded and was gone.

I sat back down and offered up a prayer of thanks.

She was still a little groggy when I was finally led to Jodi in recovery. "Hey, gorgeous," I said when I saw her.

"I doubt that," she said.

I kissed her on the forehead. "I'll be the judge of that. How are you feeling?"

"Like someone cut me and stuck something inside me."

"Are you in pain? Want me to find the nurse?" I started back out of the room.

"Come here. I'm okay."

I pulled a chair closer to the bed. "Did they tell you anything yet?"

"No. The doctor will be in in a little while. That's all I know."

"Everything went as expected," the doctor said when he came by much later. He filled us in on what we needed to know. Watch for infection, pick up a prescription for painkillers, be sure to go for the scheduled scans and make an appointment to see him in two weeks.

The recovery nurse showed up with a wheelchair and I went to get the car. The ride to the drugstore for meds and then to Jodi's apartment was quick and the traffic light. I helped her up the few steps to her building and helped her settle on the couch in her apartment.

"Hungry?" I asked.

"Not really. I think I could use a pain pill."

I pulled the bottle out of my purse and read the directions. "It says it may cause nausea if not eaten with food." I opened the bottle and spilled a couple of pills into the palm of my hand.

"How about wine? Does it cause nausea with wine?"

"Aren't you just so funny?"

"Why yes. Yes, I am."

I didn't know if her mood was a sign that her attitude was better or if the medication they gave her at the hospital still had her a little loopy. She didn't say much on the car ride home, so I wasn't sure.

"Do you feel like some toast?"

"Why? Do I look like some toast?"

I couldn't help but giggle. "A little around the edges. Yes." I went into the kitchen to search for some bread. She had fallen asleep sitting up by the time I had the toast made. It was all I could do not to go to her and kiss her.

Jodi

I woke the next morning feeling like someone had hit me in the gut with a baseball bat. There was a single pain pill and a glass of water on my nightstand. I sort of remembered Beth mentioning it was there when I needed it. There was a shiny silver bell with a black wooden handle next to the glass of water. My memory slowly seeped back into my brain. I was supposed to ring that if I needed anything. Beth said she would come running. I attempted to sit up, but that increased my pain level to an unbearable level. I considered trying to swallow the pill without water, but that didn't seem like a feasible plan. My luck I would choke on it. I had no choice but to ring the bell. I wasn't sure what time it was, I couldn't see the clock. I hoped I wasn't waking Beth up.

"Hey, sleepyhead." Beth came in wiping her hands on a dish towel. "How ya doing?"

She must have read the expression on my face.

"Not so good, huh?" She glanced at the pill still on the nightstand. "Time for this?"

"I'm thinking that would be a hell of a good idea. But it hurts to sit up."

"Do you have any straws?"

I shook my head.

"Want me to help you sit up?"

"Yeah."

Beth sat on the edge of the bed and slipped an arm under my neck. I lifted my shoulders so she could get her arm around me better. It felt so good to be this close to her. I forgot my pain for a moment—almost.

I couldn't do much to help her. Engaging my abdominal muscles hurt like hell. She was much stronger than I thought and had little trouble getting me into somewhat of a sitting position. With her free hand, she got the pill and popped it into my mouth. Then she handed me the glass of water. The pill went down with no problem and I couldn't wait for it to kick in.

"Oh, Sam called after you were asleep last night to see how you were doing," Beth said. "I hope you don't mind that I answered your phone."

"Of course not."

"I gave him my number so if he calls again and you're sleeping it won't bother you," Beth said. "This is cozy."

A little too cozy. I realized I was resting my head on her shoulder and her head was resting on mine. I sat up a bit more and was hit with a wave of pain and nausea. I gave myself a moment to assess whether I was in danger of throwing up. I decided I wasn't.

We stayed like that for several long minutes. I didn't want the feelings it was stirring in me, and I was afraid it might be stirring the same feelings in Beth. I didn't want to lead her on in any way. Even though I was more hopeful, my future was still not certain. I didn't intend to end up in her arms only to leave them empty if I didn't make it.

"Want me to help you up or do you want to lie back down?" she asked.

"I think I need to lie down until this pill kicks in."

She gently pulled the other pillow over, propped it behind me, and helped me back to a semi-lying position. "How about I make you breakfast? I can bring it in here if you can't come out."

"I think I need to sleep a little more until some of this pain subsides."

"Of course." She kissed me on the forehead, then left the room. My skin felt warm where her lips had been.

I wasn't sure how long I had slept, but my pain was much improved when I woke up. I tentatively sat up. Yep. Much better. I did everything in slow motion, swinging my legs off the bed, standing, walking to the living room.

Beth was sitting on the couch with her laptop open. I could see she was on the internet and a page that said *Pancreatic Cancer* on top was visible. She closed the laptop as soon as she saw me.

"How are you doing?" She stood and set the computer on the coffee table in front of her.

"Better."

"Sit. I'll make you something to eat."

I did as I was told. "I really appreciate everything you're doing for me, Beth." I truly did.

"Of course," she said, like it was not a big deal, and disappeared into the kitchen.

Beth stayed for four days, sleeping on my couch at night. The last night she was there, I got up to use the bathroom and snuck a peek at her while she slept. Her hair was a tangled mess. Bits of mascara in uneven smudges were visible under her closed eyes. With her mouth slightly open, her even breathing was just short of a snore. She was the most beautiful sight I had ever laid eyes on. My breath caught in my throat. I stood staring for several minutes before making my way back to bed. I fought to go back to sleep and erase the image of the sleeping beauty from my mind. I needed to distance myself from these feelings. There was still a big chance that I wouldn't survive, and I didn't want to make things harder for her if I didn't. But it was getting harder and harder to convince myself that keeping her at a physical and emotional distance was the best idea.

Beth

To my surprise, Jodi told me to get back to my life several days after her surgery. I had been leaving my salon for Cindy to run. Maybe it *was* time to get back to work. Jodi insisted she was doing well enough to manage on her own. I had no choice but to believe her.

"You're absolutely sure you can cope?" I asked her. I really didn't want to leave. Even though there had been nothing physical between us, other than me giving her an occasional kiss on the cheek or forehead, I liked playing house with her. Making her meals, adjusting her pillows, and helping her into bed at night. The first night, I helped her out of her clothes and into her pajamas. I averted my eyes as I did it. Afraid that if I really looked at her naked body I wouldn't be able to look away, or worse yet, I would be tempted to touch her. I felt I had done good keeping the distance between us that she seemed to be insisting on. I wasn't giving up. But I knew I needed to give her some time to heal before I put forth a full out effort to win her back.

My bag was packed and I was ready to go. I gave Jodi a hug, careful not to squeeze too hard and hurt her.

"Beth, I really appreciate everything you've done for me," she told me for the hundredth time.

"I'll call you later to check on you. Let me know, day or night, if you need anything."

She nodded.

"I mean it. You call me for anything."

"I will." She held up her hand holding her first two fingers away from her other two fingers. "Scout's honor."

"That's the sign for live long and prosper from Spock."

She shrugged. "That works too."

I laughed. I wanted to hug her again but held off.

She held the door open for me and I could tell she was watching me as I went down the hall. I turned and gave a small wave before turning the corner.

I stopped at the salon before heading home. I hadn't been to work since Jodi's surgery but felt comfortable leaving it in Cindy's hands.

"Hey, boss," she said when I walked through the door. Several clients sat in the waiting area, and all three of my employees had a client in their chairs.

"Busy here. I like it." I glanced at the scheduling book and decided to stay and help out. It looked like we had a steady stream of clients coming in.

Even though it had only been a few days, it felt good to have scissors in my hand chatting away with the person in my chair.

"How's Jodi feeling?" Cindy asked me when things quieted down. I filled her in. "She's a tough lady. I think she'll be fine."

I didn't even want to think about the alternative. There was no way I could lose Jodi. The times we spent apart, she was never far from my mind. I regretted those times and letting our time together—even as friends—slip away. I vowed never to let that happen again. Jodi was important to me, and I wanted to spend the rest of my life showing her that. I just hoped I had plenty of time to do that.

Maddie was out when I got home. She'd been looking for her own place but hadn't found what she was looking for. I was glad for the alone time. I put my bag in my room to unpack later, poured myself a glass of wine, and put my bare feet up on the edge of the coffee table. I had only been away from Jodi for several hours, but I missed her already. I pulled my phone from my pocket and hit her name in my contacts.

"Miss me yet?" I said, trying to be silly, but also trying to gauge her feelings.

"Did you go somewhere?"

Damn, not the response I wanted. But it was probably a good sign that she was being her usual smart-ass self. "Nope. I'm calling you from your bathroom."

"Well, come on out. I've been waiting to pee."

"How are you feeling?"

"I'm okay. Was a little nauseous earlier, but the doctor said that was a possibility." I had been afraid that some of the side effects could be a problem.

"Did you eat?"

"Yes, Mom."

"Okay, smarty. I'm just making sure. How's the pain level?"

"Much better today. Still tender to the touch."

"Then I suggest you don't touch it."

"Good thinking. Did you eat?"

I realized I hadn't. My stomach growled as if on cue.

"Well?"

"Well is for horses."

"It's hay is for horses. Well is for water. And don't change the subject. You didn't eat, did you? You are much better at taking care of other people than you are at taking care of yourself."

"I stopped at the salon and they were busy, so I stayed and helped."

"Helping other people at your sacrifice is one thing. Helping others at your detriment is a whole other thing."

"Good point. I'll try to remember that." I got up to go see if there was any food in the refrigerator.

"Bullshit. You won't remember. I know you." She did. She knew me probably better than anyone else ever had. That's one of the things I loved about her. She saw me and she paid attention.

"I'm getting something to eat right now. Happy?" To my surprise, there was a plate in the fridge covered with tin foil and a note on top. *Mom, I thought you might be hungry when you got home. Love ya!* I lifted the foil to discover a pork chop, mashed potatoes, and green beans. My daughter had grown into quite the thoughtful adult. "In fact, Maddie made me a plate of food. I'm putting it in the microwave even as we speak."

"Yes. I'm very happy."

I doubted that. She had acted grateful, but she definitely hadn't acted happy. "Good. I would do anything to make you happy. You know that, don't you?"

She ignored the question. "You should eat and then relax. You've gone above and beyond the last several days. You deserve some time to yourself."

I put the plate of food in the microwave, sans the tin foil, and pressed a couple of buttons. "I liked taking care of you." Okay, time to stop letting her know in these not so subtle comments that you want her. "I plan on taking a hot bath after I eat and heading to bed."

No answer.

"Jodi?"

No answer.

I could still here background noises so I knew we hadn't been cut off. I didn't hear her drop the phone, but that didn't mean she didn't pass out. I set the plate I had just taken out of the microwave on the counter, grabbed my car keys, and was as far as the front door ready to run over there, when Jodi came back on the line. I stopped in my tracks.

"Sorry about that," she said.

"Are you okay?"

"I think so." She cleared her throat. "Hold on. I need to get some water."

I tapped my foot nervously while I waited for her to come back.

"I just threw up."

"What?"

"Throw up, vomit, puke."

I shook my head. Why did she have to act like an ass? "I know what it means. Were you feeling sick?"

"No. It just came on all of a sudden."

"How do you feel now?"

"I'm not sure. I still feel kind of sick to my stomach."

"I'm coming over," I said.

"No, you aren't. This is your first night in several to be in your own bed. My couch can't be that comfortable. I'm fine. You stay home." To call her stubborn would have been an understatement. I considered ignoring her orders and going over there anyway. "Beth," she said. "Are you listening to me? Put your keys down and go eat. Don't come over here."

"Get out of my head." I hung my keys up on the key rack by the door.

"Why? I like it in there. It's very spacious."

I made my way back to the kitchen and my food. "Is that an insult?"

"I'll never tell. Now go eat some dinner. I'll talk to you later."

Reluctantly, I hung up the phone. My worrying was starting all over again.

Jodi

I didn't let on to Beth, but that sudden bout of sickness really scared me. I had no warning and barely made it to the bathroom before my stomach exploded out of my mouth. I headed back in there to wipe up a few splash spots. My insides were rumbling and my incision hurt.

I knew vomiting was a possible side effect of the clinical trial, but I never expected it to come on so fast without warning. I hoped this wasn't the start of something.

I brushed my teeth, rinsed my mouth several times with mouthwash, and got my pajamas on. It was still fairly early in the evening, but I thought lying down and getting some extra rest might be a good idea.

I fell asleep right away but had a restless night. My stomach felt off, sort of nauseous, sort of a dull ache. I chalked it up to the vomiting episode. It continued through the morning, and I decided to forgo coffee and have a couple of pieces of dry toast. The bland food choice didn't make a difference, and the toast came up about thirty minutes after I ate it.

I really hoped it was a stomach bug, but I was pretty sure it was a side effect from the medicated disc that was implanted in me. Shit. I knew I shouldn't have let my guard down and allow myself to start to feel hopeful. I considered calling the doctor or Beth but decided against it. I would deal with this on my own for a while and see how it shook out.

I took myself for a walk midday, keeping my head down so I didn't have to interact with anyone. The last thing I wanted to be was pleasant.

Back in my apartment, I made myself some rice, added a little cooked hamburger that Beth had prepared, and added a tiny bit of butter. I sat in front of the TV and turned on a mindless game show.

I ate slowly, conscious of how my stomach felt and prepared to stop at the slightest sign of trouble. I finished the food, placed the bowl in the sink, and drank a half glass of water. There were no signs of any digestive issues as I grabbed the lesbian romance I had been reading and settled down on the couch with it.

I drifted off to sleep around chapter nine. I woke with mild pains in my stomach. They were a little stronger than the pain that originally sent me to the doctor. I sat up and rubbed my abdomen as if that would help. It didn't.

The pain continued, coming in waves until early evening. I skipped dinner but decided on a light snack before bedtime. Beth called after she got done with work to check in. I didn't tell her about the pain or the vomiting in the morning. I feigned fatigue and told her I needed to lie down, to keep the conversation short. I didn't want her worrying more than she already was.

Sam called a little while later. He was a good ex-husband. This was the third time he had checked on me since my surgery. "How are you feeling?" he asked.

"Not good," I admitted. I told him what was going on.

"Have you called the doctor?"

"Not yet."

"Jodi, what the hell are you waiting for? Call him."

"I feel a little better now than I did earlier. I'm going to see how I feel tomorrow. I have an appointment with him in a week and a half anyway."

"Jodi, do not wait a week and a half. Call tomorrow, whether you feel better or not. Promise me."

I didn't say anything. I had to think about it. There was no sense calling if I felt better.

"Promise me," he said again, but much sterner.

"Okay. Okay. I promise. But it's probably nothing."

"Let's not take any chances here. This is your life we're talking about."

A dull pain hit me dead center of my gut. I waited for it to ease up before responding. "I am well aware that this is my life." My life. How long would this be my life? Doctors. Procedures. Scans. Operations. And would it be the end of my life?

"Will you let me know what the doctor says?"

I shook my head. I really appreciated him checking on me, but the last thing I needed was him up my ass or me needing to report to him. "I'll text you."

That seemed to satisfy him and we said our good-byes.

I was halfway to the bedroom to change for the night when I made a sudden beeline for the bathroom and made it just in time. Apparently, nothing was going to stay down. Sam was right, I needed to call the doctor first thing in the morning.

I emptied the small trash can in my room into the larger one in the kitchen. I wanted something by my bed in case I couldn't make it to the bathroom in time should I have another bout in the middle of the night.

I got myself ready for bed, climbed under the covers, and thought about whether I would tell Beth what was going on or not. Reason told me I should, but my head made a good argument against it. I didn't want to drag her into this deeper than she was. She had her own life to live. I wasn't sure how long I would still have mine.

"I want you to go right to the hospital," Dr. Daniels told me over the phone after I explained what was going on.

I hadn't eaten any breakfast because my stomach protested strongly at the very thought. It probably would have just come up anyway.

"I let them know you're coming. And the scans they need to set up. I'll be there around noon to go over the results with you."

I considered calling Beth, but only briefly. I was done pulling her into my drama. I ordered an Uber, packed a few essentials in case they kept me overnight, and went outside to wait.

I sent Sam a quick text and I was on my way.

I didn't have to wait long once I was at the hospital. The scan went quick and I was ushered to a room to await my fate.

"Well," I said to Dr. Daniels once I was seated across from him.

"The medicated disc has migrated. Not much, but enough to be causing irritation to the bottom of your stomach. It is reacting every time you eat because the pressure from the food is expanding your stomach enough to make it recoil and you vomit. I don't think the medication itself it contributing to the problem."

Now that didn't sound good. I shuddered at the thought of this stray medical equipment wreaking havoc on my insides. "What do we do about it?"

"Leaving it where it is isn't an option. You won't last long if you lose your cookies every time you eat."

I smiled at his word choice, despite my anxiety.

"Best bet is to go back in and put it back in its proper place and throw a stitch in to keep it from moving again."

"So, we should leave it in? We're talking another surgery?" Damn, I was still so sore from the last one.

"Yes. Two small incisions this time. One for the…" He continued and I wished that Beth was sitting by my side to absorb all of this. My brain had been a useless pile of mush since I was first diagnosed. "Do you have any questions?"

I considered giving a smart-ass answer—as Beth would have called it—like, *When will this nightmare end?* "When should we do this?" I asked instead.

"As soon as possible. I can have you admitted now. And I'll book the OR for later today. I want you to spend at least one night, maybe more, in the hospital. I want to make sure you are holding down food, and we can give you fluids in the meantime. "Do you have anyone here with you?"

I shook my head.

"You might want to call someone. I find it's better for you if you have a support person. Let's go back to the waiting area. I'll take care of the paperwork and we'll get you admitted. Shouldn't take too long."

I plopped down in the chair to wait and sent Sam an update. I was both annoyed at him for making me report to him and happy I had someone to share this with. It seemed to take forever before someone finally brought me to my room.

My roommate was fast asleep in the other bed, mouth wide open, snoring loudly. If I had to guess I would say she was easily eighty or ninety years old. Not a good start. The person who escorted me here—I forgot what he said he was—orderly maybe—pulled the curtain closed between us as if that would make a difference. The chainsaw imitation continued.

I signed more papers, got a lovely hospital gown on, and painful IV put in my arm. I climbed dutifully into bed to wait.

"What the hell were you thinking?" I jumped at the volume and the venom being spit at me. I turned my head toward the voice. Beth stood in the doorway, hands on hips, with a look on her face that would send a coyote running.

"I...how..."

"Why didn't you call me?" She stomped over to the bed, her voice still several decibels higher than normal.

I shrank back in the bed. I had no excuse she would understand. "How did you know I was here?"

"Your ex-husband called me to see if I knew what time your surgery was. Surgery! How dare you do this to me."

"God damn it, shut the hell up," came a voice from behind the curtain. Well, at least the snoring had stopped.

Beth ignored her. "You don't want to be my lover—my girlfriend, okay. I can deal with that for now. But not even wanting to be my friend. That fucking hurts. I can't believe you shut me out like this."

I couldn't believe Beth, who was scared someone would think she was gay, was now announcing that to everyone within earshot. And she was yelling so loud I was sure that included quite a few people.

A large woman with piercing eyes and thin lips took a step into the room. The name tag on her nurse's uniform said Berta. She didn't look like anyone I would want to mess with. "Excuse me, ladies. Do we have a problem in here?" Her voice rumbled.

Beth turned. "I'm sorry. I'll keep it down."

"Uh-huh. You better or I'll be showing you the door." She spun around and disappeared out the door.

Beth continued, but with a much lower tone, the anger still evident in her voice. "I don't understand why you wouldn't call me. Are you trying to be a martyr?"

"No." The floodgate holding back my tears was ready to explode. I fought to keep my composure.

Beth's tone softened a bit. "Jodi, why?"

"I've imposed enough on you. And..."

"And what?"

I looked into her eyes and I couldn't say it. I couldn't tell her that she would miss me more after I died if I let her get too close.

"And I don't know. I don't want to be a burden."

She took my hand and looked me straight in the eye. "You—could—*never*—be a burden to me. Do you understand me?"

I hesitated.

"Never," she repeated.

I nodded. Tears cascaded down my cheeks. Beth leaned in and held me. Her shirt was soaked by the time she let me loose.

"Tell me what's going on."

I filled her in on all the details. I left out the part about how scared I was. But she was no dummy. I'm sure she figured it out.

A nurse popped in, gave me some of that *feel good, sleepy time drug*, and popped back out. I was asleep by the time they came to wheel me to the OR.

Beth

I paced the entire length of the hallway waiting for Jodi to come out of surgery. When Dr. Daniels did appear, I couldn't read the expression on his face, and panic touched the edges of my heart.

"She came through just fine," he said after a very long beat. "I'm glad she came in when she did. If she had waited much longer there was a chance there could have been some organ damage."

I was so relieved that I hugged him. He didn't seem to mind.

"Will you be tending to her once she goes home?"

I wasn't sure what Jodi would say about it, but I was going to whether she liked it or not. "Yes."

"Keep an eye on her for any changes, especially more vomiting. She needs to be able to keep food down. Make sure her eyes stay clear and white. We don't want to see any yellowing. She had a list of side effects before the first surgery. I'll make sure you get a copy too. Anything unusual, give my office a call right away."

"I will," I promised. She could expect me to be all up in her face if she didn't take care of herself—or let me take care of her. I wasn't going to let her die because she was too pigheaded to ask for help.

Jodi spent a total of three days in the hospital, and a final scan before she returned home showed the disc exactly where it should be. She was healing from the surgery, but her disposition bordered on depressed.

She was unusually quiet and not forthcoming with her feelings, even when I asked her directly. She did let me take care of her, but she seemed to somehow resent it. I did my best not to take it personally—to blame the cancer and not her. I was determined to do whatever I could for her. I had trouble pulling down the bricks in the wall she seemed to be building between the two of us. The more I observed her, the more I realized she was building a wall between herself and the rest of the world. Even phone calls to her daughter were short and superficial.

"Feel like toast?" I asked her. "Cause you look like toast."

She didn't crack a smile. "Sure. Toast would be good."

I brought her the food and sat next to her. She finished it and set the plate on the coffee table. Everything she'd eaten since the second surgery was staying down. She really was feeling better physically.

"You did great." I pointed at the plate. "Keep that shit up."

Nothing.

"Jodi, I know you've been through a lot, and having to have a second operation was disappointing. But you seem like everything is hopeless."

"I gave up hope for lent."

"Well, you screwed up on that one because lent is right before Easter and your timing is off."

She didn't respond, just kind of pursed her lips tighter.

"Look at me," I told her.

"What?"

"Look at me," I said more sternly. She slowly turned her head in my direction. "Are you feeling sick?"

"No."

"Then what's going on? You are like this beautiful butterfly, full of color and brilliance that is just fading away."

"Yeah. Well, dying will do that to a person."

I felt my anger rise but forced compassion in its place. "No. Refusing to live will do that." I grabbed the plate from the coffee table and put it in the kitchen sink. I sat at the table and let myself cry. Why wasn't she fighting for herself? It was like she had given up before giving the medicine a chance to work. How could I make her see that she was giving up way too soon?

Jodi

I could hear Beth crying in the kitchen. I felt like an ass—probably because I was an ass. I had this wonderful person trying to help me, and while I was appreciative, I really wasn't giving much back. Okay, I wasn't giving anything back. I was trying to create a distance between us. Trying to spare her feelings when—if—I didn't make it through this.

Maybe I was being stupid. She'd told me she loves me. Maybe there wasn't any sparing her feelings or saving her from heartbreak if I died. I had some thinking to do. I didn't go to Beth. I thought she needed some time away from me. I certainly would if I were her. I definitely owed her an apology.

Was she right? Was I refusing to live? I had watched my mother die. I had the same disease that killed her. I thought about the end of my mother's life. Not the last couple of weeks when she had already given all she had to give, but the time before that. Right after her diagnosis she made a commitment to herself and my dad to live the best life she could with the time she had left. I hadn't remembered that. My decision had been the opposite. I decided to lie down and wait to die. Beth was right. I had been refusing to live.

The question now was how could I turn it around and how could I make it up to her? And I was determined to do just that. To everyone. It was time to stop trying to fight this on my own. It was hard for me to admit because I was always the caretaker, but I needed someone to take care of me for a while.

Beth was still in the kitchen an hour later, but the crying had subsided. I pulled up all the courage and humility I could muster and gingerly pulled myself up off the couch. I was not only dealing with pain from the second surgery but discomfort from the first one as well. I took a deep breath and headed into the kitchen.

Beth was sitting at the table with her back to me. If she heard me come in, she didn't respond. I knew words weren't going to be enough. I leaned over and wrapped my arms around her. I put my cheek next to hers and just stayed like that for several long moments, just soaking up her heat and letting my love for her flow through me. I was hoping that she could feel that love.

"I'm so sorry," I said. "I'm an ass. Not a smart-ass. Just a regular ass."

"Yeah, you are," she said without missing a beat.

Okay, I deserved that. "Will you forgive me?"

"I don't know. I'm here for the long haul, but, Jodi…" She turned and looked at me. "You need to step up to the plate. You need to *want* to live and fight for it. I can't do this all alone."

"I know." And I did. It was time to live. I wasn't sure how I was going to go from a mindset of dying to one of living, but I was going to do my best. Maybe the first step was to let Beth in. To really let her in.

"You know *what*?" She wasn't going to let me off easy.

"I know I need to stop acting like I don't care. Because I do, Beth. I really do. I care whether I live or die. I care about you. Deeply."

"Then I forgive you."

"Thank you." It was all I could manage to say.

"I *want* to take care of you."

"That's hard for me. I'm not use to being the one needing care."

"You better get used to it because I'm not going anywhere. You can't push me away."

"Thank you," I said again. "If you ever need a kidney, I'm your gal"

She hugged me. "We are trying to keep all your organs in your body. Don't be so anxious to be giving them away."

"I was only offering it to you. It's not like I'm putting an ad in the paper for a free kidney."

"Okay then. It's been a while since you've eaten, you must be starving."

There she was stepping right back into the caregiver role. "I must look like toast."

She laughed. It was so good to hear after hearing the sound of her crying earlier.

"You look like something more substantial. How about pizza?"

"I look like pizza?"

She grabbed her phone from the table. "No, silly. I thought we could order pizza. What do you think?"

"I think I'm very lucky to have you in my life. And just for the record, I missed you terribly when you weren't."

"Ditto," she said. "Let's never do that again."

"Deal." I was feeling so much better. I wasn't exactly sure why. Nothing had changed with my illness, but Beth, in her anger, gave me a different way to look at it.

I was willing to do whatever it took to make my life count—whether that consisted of only months or many, many years. I was going to make the best of them. I still wasn't sure how close to let Beth in. She was wrapped around my heart. Could I let her be wrapped around my life as well?

Beth

Jodi had a few minor side effects from the medicine they implanted, but she was otherwise healing well. The bouts of nausea and the metallic taste in her mouth improved when she added enzymes and eliminated gluten from her diet. Her attitude was much improved, and she did as much in the way of activity as her body would allow. She was still somewhat uncomfortable from the surgeries.

She had an offer on her business but decided to turn it down. "I'm going to have to have something to do if—*when*—I get better? Right?" she said to me. I did have to promise that if she didn't make it, I would sell the business and give the money to her kids. It wasn't an easy promise to make. But I did it. The thought hurt my heart.

We'd gone to a couple of movies and a to a play. It was all I could do not to reach for Jodi's hand, but I was a good girl and kept my own hands safely in my lap. The thing I had missed the most when Jodi had pulled back, her humor, returned in full force.

I returned to work and went back to sleeping at my own house. As much as I missed waking up in the same apartment as Jodi, it was so good to sleep in my own bed instead of on Jodi's secondhand couch. Cindy was promoted to manager so I could work half days and spend the rest of the time with Jodi.

"Want to go to the mall?" Jodi asked

We had spent most of Sunday in her apartment binging *Orange is the New Black* on Netflix. I was learning all about the gay lifestyle—of women in prison anyway. Actually, I liked the kissing scenes and was pleasantly surprised that they turned me on.

"I'm going a little stir-crazy today. I thought maybe we could walk around the mall, get a little exercise."

"Sure," I said. "Let me just grab my purse."

I drove and we chitchatted along the way. I pulled in front of the main entrance and we did two laps around the mall at a slow but steady pace before deciding to check out the new bookstore.

We went our separate ways once inside. I wanted to check out the woman loving woman books. I thought a little education wasn't a bad thing. I hadn't given up on Jodi and I being together some day. And I figured I should know what I was doing. I thumbed through a couple of books, absorbing the information.

When I was finished, I went in search of Jodi. I found her in the self-help section. I looked at the title of the book she was holding, *How to Find What You're Looking For*.

"Are you looking for a man?" I joked.

"No," she answered. "I'm looking for a woman."

"I'm a woman."

She smiled. "Can I ask you a question?" she asked coyly, playing along.

"Sure."

"Are you single?"

I hesitated. Legally, not yet. In my heart, very much so. "Yes."

She plowed on. "Do you like girls? I mean…if you like girls, can I buy you a drink? And if you don't, well, can I buy you a drink?"

"You're a girl and I like you."

"Close enough."

"But you aren't supposed to drink."

She put her finger to her lip. "Shhh." She leaned forward and kissed me softly on the lips. "I'll buy you a cup of coffee then."

I was at a momentary loss for words. We were in the middle of a bookstore and she had kissed me. And I didn't care who saw it.

"Was that okay?" she asked me.

"Okay that you kissed me or was your technique okay? Yes, and oh yes. And I think you owe me a cup of coffee."

Her face lit up with a smile. I'm sure mine was just as bright. She slid her arm through mine and we walked to the coffee shop around the corner. I didn't know what the kiss meant, if it was the start of something, but I was anxious to find out.

Jodi

I know Beth was surprised by the kiss. To tell you the truth, I had even surprised myself. I was feeling closer to her every time I saw her. I stopped fighting the growing feelings and stopped pushing her away. I knew she wouldn't make the first move. She was respecting the decision I had made when she first said she wanted to be with me. I wasn't sure how far or how fast I should take this, but that kiss was definitely the first step toward finding out. I knew it was ballsy to do it in a public place, but I couldn't help myself in the moment. And Beth seemed fine with it, much to my relief.

We ordered our coffee and found a couple of comfy chairs by the window. "I'm glad we got out for a while today," Beth said.

"Me too. If it's nice tomorrow maybe we can go to the park and sit by the water after you get out of work." I sipped my coffee and decided I needed to let it cool down a little.

"Maybe we could feed the ducks. I can pick up a couple of loaves of bread."

"Oh no," I said.

"No duck feeding?"

I shook my head. "We can feed the ducks, but not bread. It's not good for them."

Beth laughed. "Just cause you're off of gluten, no one can have it?"

"I read it. Honest. I don't lie—hardly at all—anymore."

"Anymore? Good to hear. So, what do we feed them? Chicken feed?"

I tried my coffee again. Still too hot.

"Need more cream?" Beth asked and was up getting it for me before I even had time to answer. She handed me several containers, and I added two to my coffee and sipped again.

"Thank you. You take good care of me."

"You're worth it. Anyone ever tell you that?"

I thought about it for a second. Claire certainly hadn't. "Nope. Just you."

"That's cause everyone else is an idiot. Now tell me what we feed the ducks so I can pick some up."

"Cracked corn, frozen peas, or corn that's been thawed, cut grapes." I tapped my chin trying to remember what else I had read. "Oats."

"I think I have some instant oatmeal at home. Do you think they would like the apple and cinnamon flavor?"

"Are you out of your mind? They shouldn't eat that. They much prefer the maple and brown sugar variety."

Beth laughed out loud. "You're such a goof."

"That's why you love me."

She turned serious for a moment. "It is. It's one of the many reasons."

The coffee shop was filling up, I suspected the nearby movie theater had just let out. The gentle hum of conversation replaced the silence that greeted us when we first walked in. "How many reasons are there?" I asked.

She thought for a moment. "Six thousand, four hundred, seventy-two and a half."

"What's the half?"

"You squeeze the toothpaste from the middle of the tube. But you always clean any toothpaste that oozes out before you put the cap back on. Minus one for the squeeze and plus a half for the clean cap."

"You've got this down to a science, huh?"

"Pretty much." She sipped her coffee. Her tone turned serious. "Are you ready for next week?" Radiation. Five days a week for three weeks. The latest scan showed that the localized chemo they had inserted had shrunk the tumor by about ten percent. The next step, radiation, would hopefully shrink it even more. The smaller it was when they performed the final surgery to remove it the better all around. Was

I ready? I guessed so. I wasn't looking forward to it or the possibility of side effects.

I nodded. "Ready as I'll ever be to have a radioactive beam shot into my body."

"Stop it. You're turning me on."

I laughed. The mouthful of coffee I had just taken threatened to come spewing out. I managed to swallow it down without choking. I continued to laugh until I had tears in my eyes. I needed this. I needed Beth. How could I have not recognized it sooner? I had been in such denial. I think I had wanted her since the first time we sat down and had a conversation. But so much had been in our way. Most of that was gone now, but not the cancer. I sent a silent plea up to the Universe for healing so I could live my life with Beth, if she still wanted me. I realized I hadn't done that. I hadn't asked the Universe, my spirit guides, or anyone else on the other side for help with this. How utterly foolish of me to try to face this alone.

"You okay?" Beth asked. "You got very quiet there all of a sudden."

"Yep. I was just thinking."

"Care to share?"

"I was thinking how grateful I am to have you. And how wonderful you are."

"That goes both ways, my friend."

Friend. That was the category I had kept her in. Forced her to stay in. I hoped it wasn't too late to explore other possibilities.

"What do you say we blow this Popsicle stand?" I asked.

"What? What does that mean?"

"You've never heard that before? Do I have to teach you everything?"

"There's a thing or two I'm willing to let you teach me."

I was getting the feeling she hadn't changed her mind about being with me. The thought sent a tingle through me, and I was momentarily lost in the feeling.

"Well?"

"Um…"

"What does it mean?"

Oh that. I had completely forgotten the question. "It means let's get out of here."

"That's a funny way to say it." She stood, reached for my empty coffee cup, tucked it inside of hers, and offered me a hand. I accepted the help and carefully boosted myself up.

"Here we go," she said. "Blowing this Popsicle stand."

Here we go, I thought. Here we go.

Beth

It had been quite a day. Between the lesbian scenes in *Orange is the New Black* and that unexpected kiss in the bookstore, my juices were flowing. I hoped I had fresh batteries for my vibrator when I got home.

"How about I make us dinner tonight?" Jodi asked when we got back to her place.

"Are you up for it? With all the walking you did today you must be sore."

"You've been taking care of me. Let me take care of you for a change."

"If you're sure," I said reluctantly. I would have been perfectly happy to put something together for us to eat.

"You go sit. Watch TV, read a book, take a nap. Relax."

"You won't let me help?"

"I've got this. Go." She turned me around by the shoulders and patted my butt to get me moving.

I played on my phone until she set the food on the table and called me in to eat. When we finished, I insisted that she go sit and I would clean up. She didn't put up an argument, and I suspected she had worn herself out.

"All set," I said when I was finished and had joined Jodi in the living room. "I need to get going pretty soon. You must be beat and just about ready for bed."

"Are you tired?" she asked me.

"A little. Not too bad."

"Would you, um...Would you want to spend the night?"

I figured she must have overdone it with walking and then making dinner. "Sure. I didn't bring any of my stuff though."

"You can borrow whatever you need. I have a toothbrush you can use."

Of course, I would stay if Jodi needed me. "Sounds like a plan." My vibrator would have to wait. "Do you want to watch a movie?"

"Sure. Pick something out." She got up from the recliner she was sitting in and sat next to me on the couch. I was still scrolling through our choices on Netflix when she leaned toward me and kissed my cheek. I turned my head, my face inches from hers. I could feel heat radiating off of her. I tried to gauge the look in her eyes and concluded it was *want*. The same want that I was feeling. I closed the gap between us, and I put my arms around her as our lips met. Slowly. Tentatively at first. Then with more fervor and urgency. Her tongue greeted mine in a deep dance of desire. I wanted this woman. This beautiful woman. Her fingers snaked through my hair and down my back. When she brought them up again, they were inside my shirt, skimming over my skin, leaving a hot trail in their wake. She unhooked my bra and I broke contact with her lips long enough to allow my shirt to be removed. I shimmied out of my loose bra and tossed it on the floor where my shirt had landed.

She pulled back. My breath was ragged as I looked into her eyes, trying to read her face. Had she changed her mind? Was she in pain?

"I just want to look at you," she said in response to the question I hadn't verbalized. Her eyes skimmed over me, and it was as if it was her hands touching me. The sensation was the same. "You're beautiful," she said when her eyes once again met mine.

Her lips were pressed against mine before I had a chance to respond. Her fingers slid up my rib cage to my breasts. I moaned against her mouth as her expert fingers kneaded my flesh and her thumbs made gentle circles around my nipples.

She left my mouth, tilted her head down, and sucked a nipple in. The sound that came from my throat surprised me. She stopped long enough to look up at me.

"You like?"

"Oh my God, yes."

I had to hold on to the back of the couch as the feeling of her tongue dancing around my nipple left me in a puddle. The hand she slipped between my thighs was too much. I was afraid I was going to lose control and orgasm right there. I needed to slow down. My body was on fire and I needed to gain a little control.

I pulled her head up, kissed her hard, and pushed her backward on the couch. She let out a low moan and put her hands up to stop me from lying on top of her. I sat up quickly. Shit. In the heat of passion, I had forgotten about her healing incisions.

"I'm so sorry. Did I hurt you?" I had trouble spitting the words out. My heart was pounding so hard, I was certain her neighbors heard it.

"I just need a minute," she said, pulling herself to an upright position. "My fault." She rubbed a thumb over her incisions.

"Do you need to stop?" I asked. Hoping that her answer was no but telling myself it was okay if she did.

"Absolutely not. Unless you want to."

"Did I seem like I wanted to stop?"

She laughed. "No. It seems like you were getting into it. You went all animal on me there for a minute."

"I'm so sor—"

She put a finger to my lips. "Stop. I'm teasing you. I liked it. I liked it a lot."

I blew out a puff of air, trying to compose myself. My breathing had returned to normal, but the throbbing between my legs hadn't let up much.

"What do you say we continue this in my room?"

"I thought you wanted to watch a movie," I teased her.

She grabbed the remote from where it had landed when I dropped it earlier. I hadn't even realized it had left my hand and turned the TV off. "No movies tonight. I have something else in mind, that I hope will be much more entertaining." She stood and held out her hand. I took it and walked with her to the bedroom.

She turned on the small lamp on the nightstand and started to remove her shirt.

"Stop," I told her. "I want to do that." I looked into her deep green eyes, that held a hint of blue in the dim light of the room. One by one, I unbuttoned her shirt and slid my hands over her shoulders to remove it completely. I reached behind her, unfastened her bra, and released her breasts from their restraints.

I gently ran my fingers over her scars before slipping my hands into the back of her pants and cupping her ass. I pulled her toward me and kissed her lips gently. I parted them with my tongue, and all bets were off as she held my face and deepened the kiss. We were both naked and on the bed within seconds. Hands, legs, tongues, touching, exploring, wanting.

The back of her hand swept down my body from my chin, across my chest, and down my stomach to the tangle of soft hair. A single finger found its way inside the folds, and I sucked in a gulp of air. This seemed to urge Jodi onward and she slipped the finger inside me. Just the one at first, and then another. She moved them with a rhythm that seemed to match the beating of my heart. The world became a blur as lights flashed behind my closed eyelids and I shuddered with an earth-shattering orgasm.

Jodi slipped her fingers out and I let out a small whimper at their absence and how sensitive they had left me. Her body was soft and warm and oh so good, as she curled into me and held me until my breathing and heartrate slowly returned to normal.

"Wow," I said when I was finally able to speak. "I never...I mean so fast...never..." I was still having trouble getting my brain to fire out coherent thoughts.

"Sounds like you never," Jodi teased me.

"Not like that."

She kissed the top of my head and absently stroked the side of my breast. "Good."

"Good God."

"No need to call me God. Your majesty will do."

I laughed. I felt surrounded by not only her arms, but her love. It was palpable. This was so much better than my vibrator. So. Much. Better.

"You ready to get some sleep?"

"No way. Unless you need to. Cause I'm not nearly done."

"You seemed pretty done to me a few minutes ago." I could tell she was smiling even without looking at her.

"I'm not done with you."

"Oh yeah? What did you have in mind?"

"I'd rather show you than tell you."

"I can deal with that. Or you can narrate as you go."

"First," I said, pulling myself up so I was face-to-face with her. "I'm going to kiss you like this." I took her face in my hands and kissed her gently on the nose.

"Is that the best you can do?"

I ran the tip of my tongue along the edge of her top lip before plunging it into her mouth. She must have liked it because she responded immediately. "Better?" I asked when we came up for air.

"Much. What else are you going to do?"

"Just watch me." I ran a trail with my tongue down her neck to the center of her chest. Her heart picked up its rhythm as I neared her breasts. I gave each one attention in turn, sucking and licking as I went. It took me only a second to work up the courage to move downward to the destination I sought. I was on a mission.

I gently parted her folds with my fingers before tentatively exploring her center with my tongue. I was surprised and aroused by how wet she was. The moan she let out caused an unexpected cascade of sensations in my own body.

I totally let go of the fact that I had never done this before and let my instincts take over. I listened to the sounds of pleasure coming from Jodi and let that be my guide. I had hoped to give Jodi pleasure. What I didn't expect was how much pleasure it was giving me. I was in a constant state of arousal, and when Jodi arched her back and rode the wave of an orgasm, my body came close to doing the same.

I hoped this was the first of many times that we could be together like this.

Jodi

"You haven't done that before, have you?" I asked Beth when she was once again cuddled against my side.

"Done what?"

"That." I pointed downward.

"Was it that obvious?"

I kissed her softly. "No. It was that good." I was still throbbing.

"Really?"

"Really, truly." I pulled the sheet up over us. "Does this mean you're gay now?" I said, only half joking.

"Is it bad if I say no?"

My heart stopped. No? Did that mean this wasn't what she wanted after all?

"Would you say bi?"

She turned her head to look at me. "I don't think that fits either. I haven't been attracted to other women. It's just been you. I was talking to my sister about this—"

"You were?" I interrupted her.

"Yes. Why does that surprise you?"

"I don't know. I guess it makes sense you would need someone to talk to. I guess…because of the religious beliefs. Was she okay with it?"

"Actually, she was very supportive. Anyway, she thought I was pansexual."

"Does that mean you're into cooking?" I teased her.

"Yes. Exactly. I'm really into stir-fry." She ran a single finger up and down my forearm. "It means—"

"I'm just kidding. I know what it means." I could deal with that. I could deal with anything, as long as she hadn't changed her mind about being with me. "I thought maybe you were a sapiosexual. That means you were extremely attracted to my high intelligence."

"You made that up."

"Did not. I is extremely intelligent. I went to college and got me a goodly education and everything."

She laughed. "You is a big smarty all right."

"It is a real thing though."

"It is? What does it mean?

"It's finding intelligence sexually attractive or arousing."

"Oh, I definitely find your intelligence arousing. What's the word for finding your body arousing?"

"That would make you..." I pretended to think for a moment. "Smart. Extremely smart."

"Let's see. I'm attracted to your heart, your brain, and your body. Did I leave anything out?"

"My sense of humor?"

"Jodi." She looked deep into my eyes.

"Yes."

"Your sense of humor was the first thing I fell for. You are so hilarious I cream my jeans every time you say something funny."

I couldn't help but laugh. "I can't believe you just said that."

She laughed along. "Me either. You bring out the bad girl in me. I've never talked that way in my life."

"Serious question. Are you okay with everything that just happened—with what we did?"

"Serious answer—absolutely. More than okay. You? How are your incisions? Sore?"

"I forgot all about them. I think I had my mind on something else. Or maybe I couldn't focus my mind on anything. I don't really know. It was sort of an out-of-body experience. It is starting to get a bit tender though. I might need something to take my mind off it again."

"Well, if it's for medical purposes, we absolutely should do something."

That was all the encouragement I needed to pull her face to mine, plant my lips on hers, and start the medical procedure.

❖

I woke in the morning just as the sunlight began to filter through the sheer curtains of my bedroom. It took me a moment to remember that I was naked and pressed up against Beth's back. My hand was lying across the smooth, warm skin of her stomach.

I moved my fingers across her soft flesh and made lazy circles before inching my way up her chest, between her breasts and to the hollow of her throat.

I whispered her name and she stirred; a small moan escaped from the back of her throat. It vibrated under my touch. I moved my fingers with a single destination in mind. When I reached the spot I desired, a flood of wetness greeted me. Beth's hand moved on top of mine and her fingers stroked the back of my hand, as I stroked the soft, secret folds of her body.

"You're so wet, I whispered.

A moan was her only reply.

"I need to taste you."

She nodded and rolled onto her back, as I made my way down her body, stopping at her breasts and tasting the salty sweetness with my tongue. Her nipples hardened as I sucked them in, first one then the other. I continued my downward trek until I found the prize I sought. I breathed in the scent that was Beth and felt almost lightheaded from the wonder of it.

Her hips rose to meet my mouth as I plunged my tongue into her center. She tasted like I imagined heaven must be. Small sounds came from her throat, and I adjusted my movements until her volume increased.

Her fingers tangled in my hair as she pushed the back of my head down into her. I didn't need any encouragement as I pushed my tongue deeper with each push. Her legs opened wider as my movements quickened and her breath turned ragged.

I slipped two fingers into the wetness beneath my tongue. I found the spot inside her that brought her hips up off the bed, and stroked it. Her breath quickened and held as a spasm shook through her, threatening to dislodge me from my spot. I held tight as a gasp and then a groan escaped Beth's lips. I let her body dictate my movements. It knew what it needed and wanted, and I went along for the ride. Her release was quick and full.

I pulled myself up alongside her and held her tight as she came down from the ride. I planted small kisses along her collarbone and throat. When her breathing at last settled down, I moved my lips to hers.

"My turn," she said, when she had recovered enough to move. Her hands began to roam and explore my body. I could feel the pressure building as she touched me. Her hands on my breasts made me throb farther below. I wanted her. Bad. She fulfilled a dream that I had long held. Her hands, her face, her heart filled in the blank spots of that fantasy.

Her fingers found their way down to the center of my desire. They pushed their way through, and I felt my myself jerk and tighten from her touch. My heart pounded against the wall of my chest, threatening to beat right through it.

Beth's fingers found a beat and pounded out a steady rhythm. Sensations overwhelmed me. Her closeness, her breath, her touch was almost more than I could bear.

I searched the air until my mouth found hers. I needed every part of Beth touching me. Her tongue caressed the inside of my mouth, as her fingers caressed the inside of my very being.

She held tight as I broke over the crest of the wave I was riding, and the intensity of it ripped through my body. I clung to her for dear life. I felt like I was drowning in it and she was the air that I needed to breathe.

We stayed wrapped in each other's arms as sleep once again overtook us. And a peace like I've never known settled into me. I wanted to go on loving Beth forever. I was determined to live. I just hoped that her love and my determination were enough.

Beth

The week with Jodi had been amazing. I didn't know I could feel like that. So loved. So wanted. So a part of someone else. I'd only slept home one night and went back to Jodi's the next day after work with clothes and several bags of groceries.

We were about to put the romance on hold and start the radiation treatments. I knew Jodi was anxious, both to get them started and to get them over with. We were told that the treatments themselves were short, only lasting about fifteen minutes a session, and painless. But there was always the possibility of side effects. So, fear of the unknown held a space in the back of my brain as I'm sure it did in Jodi's.

Jodi came out of the bedroom dressed in a button-down dress shirt and a crisp pair of jeans. "I'm ready to go, if you are."

"Why are you so dressed up?"

"I am meeting the procedure that is going to help me back on the road to perfect health. I wanted to make a good impression." She smiled. It was so good to see her fighting this and happy to be alive again.

"Well, you look great. That radiation should be very impressed." I had taken the day off from work, leaving Cindy in charge, so I could spend the rest of the day with Jodi.

The trip to the hospital was relatively quick. The wait to get the treatment—not so much. Jodi was unusually quiet as we sat in the waiting area. I gave her hand a squeeze. "How ya doing?"

"I'll be better when this is over with."

"Want me to see what's taking them so long?" A tech in bright green scrubs called Jodi's name before she had a chance to answer. I stood up when she did and gave her a kiss. "You got this, honey." I sat back down to wait and reflected on how far I had come with Jodi, from my first thoughts of loving her and the fear it provoked. So much so that I had to bury it inside me. To now, when I could kiss her in a semi-public place. Maybe it had to do with my fear of losing her. I didn't want to miss any opportunity to show her how much I cared.

"How did it go?" I asked her when she came out.

"It was a simulation. I had forgotten that this appointment was a CT scan to locate the tumor and the exact place to aim the radiation." She lifted her shirt to show me a small mark on her skin. "Right here."

I hadn't gone with her to the appointment to discuss the radiation therapy and what to expect. I made a mental note not to miss any other appointments. It wasn't like Jodi to forget things, but she was so overwhelmed with this disease, I wasn't surprised.

"No side effects today, so if you want you can go to work after you drop me off. I wanted to work on a new design idea I have for a sign, so I'll be fine." I was happy to hear that. She'd finished the sign orders she had already started when she was first diagnosed but hadn't done any work since. It had been like she was sitting back, waiting to die.

I took her up on her offer to just drop her back off at home but decided not to go to work. I ran home, grabbed a few odds and ends that I wanted with me at Jodi's, and then headed to my mother's.

"Hi, sweetie," Mom said. I found her in the backyard, working in her garden. "No work today."

I sat in a nearby lawn chair. "No, Jodi had her first radiation appointment today."

"Oh, that's right. Let me go wash my hands. Come on in. I have iced tea in the house. You can tell me how it went."

I filled my mom in on the few details for today.

"She is so lucky to have a friend like you."

I tapped my finger on the side of my glass, avoiding my mother's eyes. "It's more than that, Mom."

"She's your best friend. I know that."

I took a deep breath and searched for the best words. I decided to dive right in. "I love her." I looked up at her to gauge her reaction.

"Of course, you do, honey."

I let out a small laugh and shook my head. This wasn't going to be as easy as I thought. But so far it would have made a great comedy routine. I started again. "I'm *in* love with her."

A look of confusion crossed her face. "What do you mean?"

I gave it a minute to sink in. I could see the cogs turning in her head and the moment she understood.

"Oh. Um…Oh."

"Yeah."

"Was it something I did?"

"What?"

"Did I not pay enough attention to you when you were growing up? Or maybe I should have remarried after your father died. You probably needed a man around to see how life was supposed to be."

"Mom. Stop. You didn't do anything. This isn't something that's wrong."

She went to the fridge, opened the door, and peered in. "I have cheesecake if you want a piece."

"Mom, sit down. I don't want cheesecake. I want to talk to you."

"How about a sandwich?"

"Should I not talk about this?"

She turned toward me. "I didn't raise you to be gay."

I didn't bother to correct her. Words and labels didn't matter. I loved Jodi, and as they say, it was what it was. She could call it what she wanted.

"Mom. Sit. Please."

She did. Silently.

"You know Jodi. She's a great person. She makes me happy."

"I don't know what you want me to say."

"I just want to know that you still love me."

She reached for my hand and held it between her hands. "Oh, honey. Of course, I love you. I will always love you. I just worry. This isn't an easy thing."

"I fought it for a long time, Mom, and I was miserable. I tried to be married. And I was miserable. It's different with Jodi. I'm happy. So happy."

"Is it because of all the men that have hurt you that you want to be with a woman now?"

"No. They have nothing to do with this."

"So, what now? Are you going to have a gay wedding?"

I couldn't help but laugh. "I think it's just called a wedding. And I don't know what's going to happen. It is way too early for that. Right now, we just need to concentrate on Jodi getting well."

The conversation took a turn to Jodi's health. The three most important people in my life now knew—and the world didn't end. I had spent so much time running from myself and from the truth that it felt like I had been holding my breath and could finally breathe. It was such a relief. Now we just had to get Jodi better. Maybe I could think of a thing or two to give her something to live for. I made a quick stop at Jen's house before going back to Jodi's. There were a few things I wanted to borrow.

Jodi

I was feeling restless after Beth dropped me off. I sat at my desk in the corner of my living room, toying with some new sign ideas. They weren't working out. The more I tried putting an idea down on paper the more frustrated I got that it wasn't working.

I heard the door open and close behind me.

"How's it going?" Beth asked.

I wasn't sure if she did it on purpose, but her voice, low and sultry, sent a chill down my spine and a surge of moisture into my underwear.

"Not good," I confessed. "It just doesn't seem to be coming today."

She sauntered up to my desk and smiled. "That's the problem. Because coming is a good thing."

"Huh?" I managed to spit out as she got closer. The silky white shirt she was wearing was slit from her collarbone to where the top of her bra would have been had she been wearing one. When had she changed out of her T-shirt and jeans from earlier? The shirt hugged her full breasts and allowed her nipples to protrude just enough to make me squirm.

"Why don't we see if we can correct that?" She gently pulled the pad of paper from my hands and tossed it on my desk. She tugged at the pen in my hand. I was so focused on her chest, inches from my face, that I didn't realize the grip I had on it.

"You're going to be needing that hand for something else," she whispered.

I released the pen. Perspiration gathered at the back of my neck. She turned my chair toward her, and straddled me. Her black, flowing skirt caught air and I realized that she wasn't wearing any underpants.

She pushed a strand of her dark blond hair from her face and tucked it behind her ear. In a single movement, she removed any space between us and circled the outside of my lips with the tip of her tongue. The shiver it sent through me settled squarely between my legs.

I slid my hands up the back of her silky shirt and pulled her head down to me. I kissed her with a hunger that had been building since the last time we made love.

She moaned loudly as I pushed my tongue between her lips and she eagerly sucked it in. Her hands were on their own mission and I found my shirt unbuttoned. Thumbs racked over my nipples through my bra, and they tightened against the fabric. I need it off, my mind screamed. I needed her hands on my skin.

Beth must have had a similar thought because she pushed my bra up and kneaded my flesh with her hands. I felt the heat from my own body reflected back at me from hers. My moans were swallowed by her eager mouth.

She pulled back long enough to look into my eyes and say, "Touch me." It was both a plea and a demand.

I pushed her skirt back to gain access to her center with my fingers. She groaned loudly as I found my target, wet and ready. She tilted her pelvis back gaining me better access. I wrapped my arm around her back keeping her firmly in place.

"I need you," she gasped. "I need you inside me."

I slipped my middle finger into her wetness and ran my thumb through her folds.

Her lips found mine again and she kissed me hard.

I slid my finger in and out of her, but I couldn't get deep enough. I pulled her in tight, and in one swift movement, I stood up with enough momentum to move her from my lap to my desktop.

She pushed a cup of pencils, paperweight and anything else in the way to the floor. I leaned her back and bent over her. I kissed her as I slipped my finger from her center. She let out a whimper of disappointment that turned to a moan as I pushed back inside of her with two fingers this time. In this position, I could more easily find what I was seeking. I found the soft spongy area swollen with her arousal. I stroked the center of her pleasure. Her mouth left mine. "Oh my God," she said, her voice husky. "Oh my God."

I moved my fingers in unison, sliding in and out just enough to keep contact with the spot. Her hips kept rhythm with me.

With my other hand, I unbuttoned her shirt. It slipped open, exposing her full breasts. I brought my mouth down to first one and then the other, sucking and lapping at the erect pink nipples.

She pulled my face back up to hers and kissed me, sweeping the inside of my mouth with her tongue. My pulsed quickened and my breath caught in my throat. I had never been kissed so thoroughly. My soul emptied into her.

She released me. Her ragged breathing told me she was getting close. I wanted my mouth on her heat when she went over the edge, and I changed my position to make it possible. I continued slipping in and out of her wetness as my tongue made its way through her velvet folds.

Her breath became ragged and her hips bucked upward as she let out a loud moan. Her muscles tightened around my fingers, and I licked her hard as the first wave of an orgasm ripped through her.

I felt my own muscles tighten and a surge of moisture as her excitement became mine. I forced myself to relax and turned my attention back to her.

"Take off your pants," she half whispered, half moaned.

I was more shocked that she could speak at all than at her request. I reluctantly slipped my fingers from her and obeyed.

She eased herself over so she was almost on her side, legs dangling over the edge of my desk. "Now come here." She pulled me closer wrapping one leg around me. Our centers met in a tangle of hair and wetness. She rubbed herself against me.

I wasn't sure I could remain standing and she seemed to sense this. She pulled at the collar of my shirt until I was bent over her.

"I won't let you go," she whispered wrapping her arms around my neck. Her hips continued to gyrate, pushing her sex against mine. Her lips met mine and she kissed me gently at first, then with more urgency as she once again edged close to coming.

Heat rose from my center through my chest and into my throat. A tear slipped from my eyes as I squeezed them shut, and I felt Beth come against me. My own orgasm ripped through me and we rocked together gathering every last drop of it until we were both spent and breathing hard.

We stayed in this position for what seemed like hours but was probably only minutes. My legs were weak, and I had trouble standing when Beth gently pushed me up.

She slid off my desk, buttoned her shirt, and smoothed her skirt down. "That should help you come up with an idea for the sign," she said. Without another word, she turned and went into the kitchen.

"Holy shit," I said out loud to no one.

❖

Anxiety moved in and settled in my stomach as I waited for my first radiation treatment the next day. Beth put her hand on my knee that I didn't realize I was nervously bouncing. I was called in rather quickly. Beth squeezed my hand, and I followed the technician back to the room. The procedure was quick. The hardest part was staying in one position without moving the whole time.

"How are you feeling?" Beth asked me once we were back at my apartment.

"Wicked tired."

"Why don't you take a nap? I'll get lunch ready and wake you up in a little while."

She didn't have to tell me twice. I made my way to the bedroom and fell asleep within minutes. It seemed like I hadn't slept at all when I was roused by Beth gently shaking my shoulder.

"Huh?"

"Jodi."

"Um. Yeah?"

"Want to get up? I've got dinner ready."

"What time is it?"

"Six o'clock. You were sleeping so deeply that I didn't want to wake you up for lunch. But you really do need to eat something. Can you get up?"

"I'm not really hungry."

"Not an option. You need to keep your strength up. Come on." She tapped my arm. "Get up."

I reluctantly did so. I picked at my food but managed to get enough down to keep Beth happy. I wasn't nauseous, just not very hungry.

The next three weeks went pretty much the same. I had my radiation treatments every morning five days a week with weekends off. At the end of each week, my tumor was scanned and measured. It was shrinking at a steady rate. At the end of the three weeks, I met with my doctor. Beth of course was by my side.

Surgery was scheduled for the end of the week. A plethora of mixed feelings coursed through me. I was anxious to get this over with. Anxious to see the outcome. Anxious to get on with my life. But fear seemed to be the predominate feeling.

Beth was great throughout the radiation treatments, making sure I ate, taking care of all the things I couldn't seem to manage because of fatigue. The fatigue also got in the way of our love life. One more reason to get this over with. The thought of making love to Beth again definitely was a great motivator.

I talked to both Annie and Andrew the day before my surgery. I still hadn't told Annie I had the same kind of cancer that had killed her grandmother. I didn't see the need to scare her. All she knew was I had a small tumor they were removing. Beth promised to call them both when I was in recovery with an update. Andrew had made special arrangements to be on base so he could take the call. It would more than likely be nighttime there.

I was getting used to the hospital prep routine, the papers I needed to sign, and my least favorite part, the IV. At least this was a real room and not a cubby surrounded by curtains.

"Doing okay?" Beth asked as she came into the room. "Home stretch."

I nodded. "I can't wait for this all to be over. I am so sick of hospitals and doctors."

"I hope you aren't talking about me." Dr. Daniels walked into the room.

"If I said yes, would you hold it against me?" I answered.

"No. I'm sick of hospitals and doctors too," he said. "But I like the nurses and orderlies."

"Yeah. They are pretty cool."

He pointed to the bag of saline dripping fluid into me. "I see they have you all hooked up and ready to go." He went over the procedure with Beth and me one more time. "They'll be up to get you in about"—he glanced at his watch—"twenty minutes. I'll see you in the OR."

"Thanks, Doc. I was just joking about being sick of you. You've been great."

"I'm glad my reputation is still intact." With a wave, he made his exit.

Beth sat close in the chair by the bed and laid her head on my shoulder. I couldn't imagine it was too comfortable. "You've come along way, honey, and it's almost over."

I stroked her hair with the hand that wasn't tethered to the IV. "Thank you for everything you've done for me. I don't think I could have gotten through this without you."

She picked her head up and looked at me. "Of course. But you could have gotten through it. You're much stronger than you give yourself credit for."

"Your faith in me makes me strong."

"Damn, woman. Take the compliment without giving me credit."

"Okay. I'm strong. I'll get through this, and we can live happily ever after."

"I would like that." She put her head back down and we stayed like that—quiet—together, until the nurse came and put a shot of something to relax me in the port in my IV line. The shot hadn't taken effect yet, when a guy in scrubs came to take me to surgery.

"I'll see you soon." Beth gave me a lingering kiss on the mouth.

"If that's what I can expect, then I'll be back before you know it."

I was feeling woozy as I was wheeled into the operating room and moved from the bed to the operating table. I was having trouble keeping my eyes open when someone placed a mask over my mouth and nose and I was instructed to count backward from one hundred. The last number I remember saying was ninety-seven. Then nothing.

I could hear someone saying my name, but my mouth didn't feel strong enough to answer and my eyes refused to open. I went back to sleep, but had no idea for how long, before I heard my name again. "Jodi. Can you wake up for me?"

I opened my eyes just enough to see who was talking to me. To say I was groggy would have been an understatement.

"Hey there. It's time to wake up, hon."

I didn't know who she was. Her thin face and horn-rimmed glasses didn't look familiar. I wished she would just leave me alone and let me sleep.

"Your girlfriend is anxious to see you."

Girlfriend? Beth? I shook my head trying to get the cobwebs dislodged. Beth. I wanted to see Beth. I must have drifted back to sleep, because when I opened my eyes again there was a totally different nurse in the room with me. She checked the machines I was hooked to and made notes in the computer.

"Where's Beth?" I managed to croak out.

"Well, hello there. You've been out a while. I'll see if she's still in the waiting area. She might have gone to the cafeteria."

I nodded. Talking was proving to be a major effort.

The nurse came back a few minutes later, followed by Beth. Beth came to the side of the bed and brushed a lock of hair away from my face. "Hi, honey. You had me all kinds of worried."

The blood pressure cuff around my arm puffed up and the machine it was attached to hummed loudly. I waited for it to stop before answering. "Why?"

"You've been asleep an awfully long time. They were having trouble waking you up."

"They should have just sent you in. I would have woken up for you."

The nurse, Marcy, her name tag said, stepped closer to the bed. "How you feeling, dear?"

She looked too young to be a nurse and definitely too young to be calling me dear.

"Tired. Thirsty." Maybe a sip of water would make it easier to talk.

She brought me a cup of water and held the straw to my lips. "Sip slowly. Not too much."

The first sip hurt to swallow, but then it eased up and the rest went down easily.

"Better?"

I nodded and turned my attention back to Beth. "Did you call the kids?"

"Not yet. I wanted to wait till you were awake. Should I call them now?"

"In a few minutes. Can you just sit with me?"

"Of course." Marcy pulled a chair up to the bed for Beth. "Thanks."

"I'll let the doctor know you're awake," Marcy said. "I'm sure he'll be in soon to see you."

We sat quietly for several minutes, which I was grateful for. I wanted Beth with me but didn't want to have to talk.

I was feeling much more alive when the doctor made his appearance. "It went well," he said. "We'll know for sure when we get the pathology report back, but the margins looked good. I think we got it all."

I wasn't prepared for the relief that washed over me. Tears sprung to my eyes. I was going to be okay. Oh my God. I was going to live. I had hoped for it, but I don't think I really believed it until that moment.

The ear to ear grin on Beth's face told the story. "That is the best news," she said. "Thank you so much." She squeezed my hand.

"As we discussed, we are going to keep you here for a few days. I want to keep a close eye on you tonight. Let's see how you are feeling tomorrow. I'll be by sometime in the afternoon. Questions?"

"How long before the pathology is back?" Beth asked.

"It usually takes anywhere from a few days to a week. I'll give you a call as soon as I have it."

I was going to live. It was time to start making actual plans with Beth.

Beth

Jodi insisted that I go into work for at least a half day instead of sitting around the hospital with her. I know she said that for my sake—and the sake of my business, but I would have gladly sat there with her, keeping her company all day. But I complied with her wishes.

"How's Jodi?" Maddie asked me as we sat down to eat breakfast together a couple of days later. It was the first meal I'd shared with her since Jodi had gotten sick.

I filled her in. "She should be going home in a couple of days."

Maddie poured orange juice into both of our glasses. "You really care about her, don't you?"

"I do. A lot. More than a lot." I passed her the plate of bacon.

She put two pieces on her plate. "I can tell."

"I told Grandma. About Jodi I mean. My feelings."

"You did?"

"Yes. I'm done hiding this. Jodi is important to me. I want her in my life."

"Wow. My mom is growing up."

I laughed. "I guess I am. Took me long enough."

"Don't beat yourself up. We are all on our own paths and some of us just take the long way around. It's not how long it takes you. It's where you end up."

"How did you get so wise?" She had come so far from those rough teenage years.

"Lots of hallucinogenics," she said with a straight face. "I'm kidding. I had a wonderful woman who taught me a lot."

"Grandma," we both said in unison. I laughed until I had tears in my eyes. Then I realized the tears were rolling down my cheeks and I couldn't stop them.

"Mom," Maddie said. "Are you all right?" She handed me a napkin.

I hadn't allowed myself to really face the fact that Jodi could have died or the relief that I felt that she was going to be okay. It all came pouring out of me at once. I nodded but the waterworks continued.

When it seemed like there were no more tears left in me, I went back to laughing. My emotions were running amok. It took a bit for me to calm down.

"That was interesting," I said, for lack of anything else to say.

"We can go with that theory. What's going on?"

"I think I was just holding everything in for so long. Trying to be strong. Guess I'm not nearly as strong as I thought."

"That is so far from the truth. Mom, you are the strongest person I know. You've been through a lot. Everything Jodi has faced, you faced with her. None of this could have been easy."

It wasn't, but I hadn't let myself be anything but a rock for Jodi. I felt like the rock had just crumbled.

Jodi's ringtone played out on my phone. I wiped the last of the tears from my face, shook my head to try to clear it, and said hello.

It wasn't Jodi's voice I heard. "Hello. Is this Beth?"

"Yes." I was confused. Why was someone else using Jodi's phone to call me?

"This is Tina. I'm Jodi Michaels's nurse for today. She asked me to give you a call to see if you could come to the hospital. She's hasn't been feeling well and had a pretty rough night."

"Oh my God, what's wrong?"

"The doctor ordered some tests. I don't believe we have the results yet."

"Of course. I'll be there as soon as I can." I stood up so fast that I knocked the chair over backward. "Jodi's sick," I explained to Maddie. "I've got to go."

"Do you want me to drive you? You look pretty rattled."

I gave it a thought, but only for a moment. "No. I'm fine. Sorry about breakfast."

"Mom, it's okay. Go. Please give me a call when you know what's going on."

I grabbed my keys from the rack by the door and headed for my car. I forced myself to keep my speed under control—if you call going fifteen miles over the speed limit controlled.

I was grateful for the valet service at the front of the hospital that allowed me to bypass the parking garage. I half walked and half ran to the elevator and up to Jodi's room. I pushed the door open, but it only opened about a foot. I realized someone was blocking it.

"Sorry. You can't come in right now." I caught a glimpse of several people gathered around Jodi's bed. I couldn't see her but could tell they were doing something to her.

"What's happening?" I just about screamed.

A nurse stepped out of the room, closing the door behind her. "Jodi's heart stopped. She is in good hands. They are doing everything they can to help her."

Oh my God. Jodi. No.

Jodi

The crushing pain in my chest was suddenly gone. I felt myself floating. No tunnel. No bright light. Just floating. I could see my body below me, a crowd of people around it. But my attention was brought upward, away from them.

I passed through colors. Swirling. Bright, like I would use on my signs. I looked down at my arm to see if the "paint" had stuck to it. That's when I noticed my arm was no longer solid. It was translucent. I could feel the lightness of it—the lack of density and some of its form.

I continued my upward trek. It wasn't a rush. It was slow and soft and gentle, and I could feel love radiating all around me, coming from everything and nothing. The softest tones played in the background echoed by sounds in my head just as melodious.

I floated into a room filled with people; their faces were fluffy and distorted at first, one by one, they came into focus. Suddenly, there was my mother. It had been almost four years since I'd last laid eyes on her. Of course, I wasn't really laying my eyes on her. I was seeing her with pure consciousness. I saw her in all her divine glory. She glowed from the inside out and it was beautiful.

My mother motioned for me to turn and look down. I did as she wordlessly instructed. There was Beth, standing outside the room where they were working on my body. She looked like she was crying. I knew in that moment I had a choice. I could stay with my mother, or I could return—to Beth—to my children—to my life.

I turned back toward my mother and saw her fade into nothingness.

❖

I struggled to open my eyes. The bright light in the room was too much to open them fully so I settled for squinting. Something squeezed my arm, and I realized it was the blood pressure cuff. When had they put that back on me? Why was my chest so sore? What was that beeping sound?

Beth got up from the chair by the bed and stuck her head out the door. I hadn't even seen her come in.

"Nurse. Nurse. She's waking up." She came back to the bed and took my hand. "Jodi. It's me. I'm here."

Of course, she was here. I'd had surgery and she'd been here every day since. But something was different. I managed to open my eyes a little wider. The room was different. Why was I in a different room? Something didn't make sense here.

I opened my mouth to ask Beth what was going on, but it came out as more of a croak. Before I could try again, a nurse was on the other side of the bed. "Welcome back."

Back from where?

She looked at Beth. "I've notified the doctor. He'll be here soon." She checked the monitors that were hooked up to me. "Everything looks good," she said to Beth.

Hey. I'm here. Someone want to tell me what's going on? But I didn't have the strength to say it out loud.

"Thank you," Beth said to the nurse, without taking her eyes off me. "You had us pretty scared," she said to me. She wet my lips with one of those little pink sponges on a stick.

"What happened?" I managed to squeak out.

"Your heart stopped. I guess it happens sometimes after surgery. But they got it going again."

That explained the way my chest felt. "Sorry I scared you."

"You need to knock this crap off. I'm not sure how much more *my heart* can take."

I smiled. I could feel the muscles in my face struggling against fatigue to hold on to it. "Come closer," I told her. My voice didn't seem loud enough to reach her.

She leaned closer and lifted my hand. "What?" she whispered.

"If I don't make it I want you to know I got my happily ever after. I got to spend the rest of my life with you." As weak as I felt in the moment, I couldn't imagine going on. I just wanted to close my eyes again, but I forced them to stay open.

"Stop that. It isn't over yet."

"I had stopped believing in fairy tales. But you made all my dreams come true." I swallowed down the lump that was forming in my throat. "I'm sorry if you don't get a happily ever after."

She leaned in even closer. "What are you talking about? You are my happily ever after."

"I mean just in case." I wasn't sure I was making sense. I just wanted her to know how happy I'd been with her.

"The only thing I regret is not figuring out sooner that it's you I should have been with." She kissed me on the forehead.

I tilted my head back, just far enough to look into her eyes again. "Hey. No regrets. We might not have started on the same page, but we certainly finished right where we were supposed to."

"We aren't nearly finished. Do you know how much I love you?"

I nodded. "Ditto."

"Sometimes the depth of that love still surprises me." She let go of my hand long enough to grab the glass of water from the side table. She held the straw while I took a sip. It helped.

"You should find someone else to love if I don't make it through this."

She put her finger over my lips. "Shh," she said. "I don't want you to talk like that."

I reached up to stroke her cheek and winced as the IV in my arm pulled. "I don't want you to be alone. You're too wonderful for that."

"Stop. You need to just stop. You're going to be fine."

I wanted to believe her. I remembered glimpses of the other side. Of my mother. I wanted to share them with Beth, but I needed to sort them out in my own mind first.

"I can see the wheels turning in that pretty little head of yours. What's going on?"

"In my head? Nothing."

"You are so full of shit."

"I'm full of a lot of things. Shit just happens to be one of them." I could feel some of my strength inch back, and I felt a little more aware—a little more with it.

"The biopsy came back. They had clean margins around the tumor."

It took a few moments to sink in. Beth must have read the confusion on my face.

"Are you getting what I'm saying? You're cancer free. All gone."

"What? It's gone?" Gone? That bit of wayward cells that threatened to take my life was gone?

"Yes."

"The kids…"

"They know about the heart attack. Andrew is actually on his way home. Sam told Annie what's going on. Maddie is picking them up from the airport…" She pulled her cell phone from her pocket and glanced at it. "In about two hours."

Beth

Jodi had fallen back to sleep by the time Sam and Annie got there. I gave them both a hug.

"How's she doing?" Sam asked. He was tall with broad shoulders. His brown hair had a bit of a reddish tint and hung a little over his ears. My first thought was that he could use a haircut. I silently laughed at myself. Occupational hazard, I guessed.

"Much better. She was awake and talking a little while ago." I gently shook her shoulder. "Jodi. You've got company."

"Mom?" Annie said. She'd grown at least a foot since I'd seen her last. She'd grown more beautiful as well.

Jodi's eyes popped open at the sound of her daughter's voice. "My baby."

"Still not a baby," Annie said with a little giggle.

"You'll always be my baby." She looked at Sam and mouthed *thank you.* He nodded.

I stepped back to give them space for their family reunion.

"Are you going to be okay, Mom?"

"I didn't think so at first, Annie. But now I'm sure I am. Just gonna take me a little time to heal." Jodi caught my eye and smiled. Annie was just the prescription she needed.

"How's that new puppy?" Jodi asked her.

"He is so cute, Mom. Want to see a picture?" Annie pulled her cell phone from her pocket and proceeded to show off her new pet, giving the exact location for each photo and what the puppy was doing.

The nurse came into the room to check vitals. "I hate to do this, but hospital rules say only two visitors allowed at a time on the cardiac floor."

"I'll go," I said. "I haven't eaten all day anyway and the cafeteria is calling my name."

"You must be really hungry to be answering that call," Sam said.

I laughed. "I've eaten in the hospital cafeteria enough times to know what to eat and what to stay away from. The pizza isn't too bad if you like cardboard."

"I love cardboard. Mind if I join you? Give these two"—he gestured toward Jodi and Annie—"a chance to catch up."

"Not at all," I said. "I'll be back soon," I said to Jodi.

To my surprise, she pursed her lips. I gave her a quick kiss and we were on our way.

"Sorry about that," I said, feeling a little self-conscious.

"You mean the kiss? No worries. Jodi and I were over a long time ago. I know how she feels about you. I'm not sure she would have made it through all this without you. I have the feeling she would have given up." I had the feeling he could still read her after all these years. "How is she really?"

"The doctor said she is doing good considering everything she's been through." I pressed the elevator button. "I have to admit I was scared to death when I got here and they were working on her, trying to revive her. They actually lost her at one point but were able to bring her back—obviously."

He let out a small laugh. "Nothing is obvious with Jodi."

I shook my head. "I'm getting better at figuring her out, but you're right. If she doesn't want to share something or let on about how she's feeling, she's good at hiding it."

We didn't have to wait long for the elevator, and the ride down to the second floor was fairly crowded. We waited until we were once again walking down the hall to finish our conversation.

"She cares about you a lot. You know that, don't you?"

I smiled and shook my head. "I do now, but that's something she was really good at hiding for quite a while. But then again, I was doing the same thing. I'm glad we are passed all that crap now."

"Me too. I'm glad Jodi has you." He held open the cafeteria door for me.

Me too. I thought. Me too.

Jodi

I was sick of being in the hospital. It had been four days since my heart attack and I was doing well. No permanent damage, they told me.

Beth had opened her home to Sam and Annie. Annie and Beth came to see me every day. Sam popped in a few times. Even Maddie and Beth's mom came to see me. But the visits couldn't keep me from going stir-crazy.

"Hey there." Beth stuck her head in the door. "I've got a surprise for you."

My crappy mood lightened. "Well, come in here and give it to me. I could use a surprise."

"Are you sure your heart is strong enough for a big surprise?" My mind went immediately to sex. It had definitely been too long. But seeing I was still in the hospital I didn't think that was what Beth had in mind.

"I'm sure. What it is?"

She let the door close for a second. I couldn't imagine what the surprise could be. She stepped back in, but the only thing she had was her iPhone. "Hold on. Let me get the video recording." She fiddled with her phone. "Okay, got it." She pointed the camera at me.

"What are you doing? I look like crap."

"You look beautiful," she said to me. "Okay, bring the surprise in," she said louder.

The door opened and in walked Andrew, dressed in camo fatigues with his duffel bag flung over his shoulder. "Hi, Mom."

Tears flooded my eyes. "Andrew. Oh my God. Andrew." I put my arms out to him. He dropped his duffel bag and came into my arms. I held him as tight as I could. My boy had become a man.

He sat on the edge of the bed. It was so good to see him. I had been so wrapped up in all the surgeries and treatment that I didn't realize how much I had missed him and Annie.

Beth slipped her phone back in her pocket. "Want me to give you some alone time?"

"No. It's fine," I told her.

"Stay," Andrew said. "How are you doing?" he asked me.

Beth sat in the reclining chair in the corner.

"I'm doing good. Cancer free."

"How long do you have to stay in the hospital?"

"I don't know. Not too much longer I hope. The doctor should be coming around soon. I plan on begging him to let me leave." I couldn't believe he was sitting here with me. He had been across the world a few days ago.

"How was your trip?" Beth asked him.

He turned so he could answer her. "It was okay. Part cargo plane, part airliner. It was just mostly long."

"I can imagine," she said.

The door flung open and Annie strutted in. "Andrew!" she said and flung herself at him. He caught her in his arms and stood to hug her. "When did you get here?"

"Just a little bit ago. How ya doing, kiddo?"

"Great."

Beth stood. "I'll go. So you can have your kids."

"Please stay," I said.

"Yes. Don't go." Annie crossed over to her and gave her a hug.

"They have rules," she said to Annie.

"The hell with the rules," I said. "I want my whole family to be here with me. And you are *all* my family. Andrew, there are chairs in the hallway. Would you mind getting one, please?"

"Sure." He disappeared for a few seconds and returned with a chair. In his absence, Annie climbed up on the bed with me. I moved over so she could stretch her legs out. Andrew set the chair next to Beth and sat down.

"Nice haircut," Annie said to Andrew. He ran his hand over his buzz cut. "How long can you stay?"

"The good news is I don't have to go back to Japan. My stint was over at the end of this month anyway, so they said I didn't have to go back. I'll be stationed in Wilkes-Barre for a year."

"Where the heck is that?" Annie asked.

I couldn't contain my smile. "It's in Pennsylvania, Annie. Less than four hours away."

"Yep. Close enough to come home for holidays." Andrew said.

"Knock, knock." Dr. Daniels pushed the door open and stuck his head in. If he noticed that we had one extra person in the room, he didn't say anything. "Ready to go home, Jodi?"

"Are you kidding me?" I responded.

"Would I joke about something like that? I'm guessing you're getting sick of the room service around here. I went over your chart on the computer and everything is looking good. I've signed the paperwork, and someone will be around shortly to go over everything with you."

"Wow. Thank you so much."

"Thank you. Your recovery has been great for my professional reputation."

"Glad I could help."

"I expect to see you in my office within the next couple of weeks."

"I'll make sure of it," Beth said.

It was another hour before the nurse came in with my discharge papers, prescription, and my instructions for home. Beth went to get the car and I changed into real clothes and was wheeled down to the main entrance followed by Annie and Andrew.

Andrew opened the passenger side door and helped me in. He and Annie jumped in the back.

Beth rubbed my knee. "Ready, honey?"

I was. I was ready to begin my life anew. I had the love of my life next to me, my two children in the back seat, and I was heading home. Absolutely nothing could have been better.

Epilogue

Beth

"Take this box," I told Jodi. "It's light."

"Stop treating me like an invalid. It's been a whole year since I was in the hospital." She was right of course, I needed to stop babying her. She had healed from the surgery and from the heart attack. There were no signs of cancer in her scans. She was totally capable of bringing in the last of the boxes from her car. The movers had already delivered the furniture, but she had insisted on packing personal items and bringing them over herself. I couldn't argue with her, seeing as I had pretty much done the same thing.

I set the box I was carrying on the couch and looked around. The house was bigger than the one I'd just left—Maddie would be staying on there. And much bigger than Jodi's little apartment. It was *our* house. We'd picked it out together, and when we showed Annie, via Skype, where her room would be, she was all for it. She had one more week with her father for the summer, which meant Jodi and I had seven whole days alone.

"Help me make the bed," I said.

"Right now?" she asked. "I was going to put dishes away."

"Yep. Right now. Come on. The box with the bedding is already in there." I took her hand and led her upstairs to what would be our room. I ripped the tape off the top of the box marked SHEETS AND BLANKETS.

I threw a fitted sheet to Jodi and dug out the top sheet and pillowcases. She started on one side while I opened another box and retrieved the pillows, blanket, and bedspread.

"What do you think?" she asked me as she smoothed down the spread.

"I like it. Now let's mess it up."

"What?"

"Take all your clothes off and climb in. Let's mess it up." She started to unbutton her shirt. "No. Wait."

"You're making me a little crazy here, woman."

"If you're crazy, don't blame me. You were a little off when I first met you."

She laughed.

I went around to her side of the bed—the brand-new bed—bought just for us. "Let me." I unbuttoned each button, stopping in between to kiss each newly exposed section of skin on her chest. I slowly undressed her and felt the moisture in my center grow as each piece of clothing fell to the floor and I caressed her.

Together we removed my clothing. I kissed her. Nothing stood in the way of our bodies becoming one as we stood in each other's arms.

I pushed her back onto the bed, and in an instant, I was on top of her, my thigh between her legs. I ran my hands through her hair, and her tongue hungrily entered my mouth.

She let out a gasp as I pulled my thigh away and replaced it with my fingers. I could feel her juices, slick and warm. We completely and thoroughly christened the bed. I felt whole and one with Jodi. Our lovemaking had become more than a physical journey. It was as if my soul was making love to her soul.

I had placed my heart in Jodi's hands because somehow, I knew I could trust her with it. And she had trusted me with her heart and her body as well. I had no intention of ever letting her down. I whispered into her ear as we drifted off to sleep. "I love you. You *are* my happily ever after."

About the Author

Creativity for Joy Argento started young. She was only five, growing up in Syracuse, New York, when she began drawing. Rochester is now home, and oil paints are her medium of choice. Her award-winning art has found its way around the globe. Her love of lesbian romance inspired her to try her hand at writing a little later.

Joy has three grown children and four grandsons who are the light of her life.

You can check out Joy's art at www.artbyjoy.com

Books Available from Bold Strokes Books

Aurora by Emma L McGeown. After a traumatic accident, Elena Ricci is stricken with amnesia leaving her with no recollection of the last eight years, including her wife and son. (978-1-63555-824-1)

Avenging Avery by Sheri Lewis Wohl. Revenge against a vengeful vampire unites Isa Meyer and Jeni Denton, but it's love that heals them. (978-1-63555-622-3)

Bulletproof by Maggie Cummings. For Dylan Prescott and Briana Logan, the complicated NYC criminal justice system doesn't leave room for love, but where the heart is concerned, no one is bulletproof. (978-1-63555-771-8)

Her Lady to Love by Jane Walsh. A shy wallflower joins forces with the most popular woman in Regency London on a quest to catch a husband, only to discover a wild passion for each other that far eclipses their interest for the Marriage Mart. (978-1-63555-809-8)

No Regrets by Joy Argento. For Jodi and Beth, the possibility of losing their future will force them to decide what is really important. (978-1-63555-751-0)

The Holiday Treatment by Elle Spencer. Who doesn't want a gay Christmas movie? Holly Hudson asks herself that question and discovers that happy endings aren't only for the movies. (978-1-63555-660-5)

Too Good to be True by Leigh Hays. Can the promise of love survive the realities of life for Madison and Jen, or is it too good to be true? (978-1-63555-715-2)

Treacherous Seas by Radclyffe. When the choice comes down to the lives of her officers against the promise she made to her wife, Reese Conlon puts everything she cares about on the line. (978-1-63555-778-7)

Two to Tangle by Melissa Brayden. Ryan Jacks has been a player all her life, but the new chef at Tangle Valley Vineyard changes everything. If only she wasn't off the menu. (978-1-63555-747-3)

When Sparks Fly by Annie McDonald. Will the devastating incident that first brought Dr. Daniella Waveny and hockey coach Luca McCaffrey together on frozen ice now force them apart, or will their secrets and fears thaw enough for them to create sparks? (978-1-63555-782-4)

Best Practice by Carsen Taite. When attorney Grace Maldonado agrees to mentor her best friend's little sister, she's prepared to confront Perry's rebellious nature, but she isn't prepared to fall in love. Legal Affairs: one law firm, three best friends, three chances to fall in love. (978-1-63555-361-1)

Home by Kris Bryant. Natalie and Sarah discover that anything is possible when love takes the long way home. (978-1-63555-853-1)

Keeper by Sydney Quinne. With a new charge under her reluctant wing—feisty, highly intelligent math wizard Isabelle Templeton—Keeper Andy Bouchard has to prevent a murder or die trying. (978-1-63555-852-4)

One More Chance by Ali Vali. Harry Basantes planned a future with Desi Thompson until the day Desi disappeared without a word, only to walk back into her life sixteen years later. (978-1-63555-536-3)

Renegade's War by Gun Brooke. Freedom fighter Aurelia DeCallum regrets saving the woman called Blue. She fears it will jeopardize her mission, and secretly, Blue might end up breaking Aurelia's heart. (978-1-63555-484-7)

The Other Women by Erin Zak. What happens in Vegas should stay in Vegas, but what do you do when the love you find in Vegas changes your life forever? (978-1-63555-741-1)

The Sea Within by Missouri Vaun. Time is running out for Dr. Elle Graham to convince Captain Jackson Drake that the only thing that can save future Earth resides in the past, and rescue her broken heart in the process. (978-1-63555-568-4)

To Sleep With Reindeer by Justine Saracen. In Norway under Nazi occupation, Maarit, an Indigenous woman; and Kirsten, a Norwegian resister, join forces to stop the development of an atomic weapon. (978-1-63555-735-0)

Twice Shy by Aurora Rey. Having an ex with benefits isn't all it's cracked up to be. Will Amanda Russo learn that lesson in time to take a chance on love with Quinn Sullivan? (978-1-63555-737-4)

Z-Town by Eden Darry. Forced to work together to stay alive, Meg and Lane must find the centuries-old treasure before the zombies find them first. (978-1-63555-743-5)

Bet Against Me by Fiona Riley. In the high stakes luxury real estate market, everything has a price, and as rival Realtors Trina Lee and Kendall Yates find out, that means their hearts and souls, too. (978-1-63555-729-9)

Broken Reign by Sam Ledel. Together on an epic journey in search of a mysterious cure, a princess and a village outcast must overcome life-threatening challenges and their own prejudice if they want to survive. (978-1-63555-739-8)

Just One Taste by CJ Birch. For Lauren, it only took one taste to start trusting in love again. (978-1-63555-772-5)

Lady of Stone by Barbara Ann Wright. Sparks fly as a magical emergency forces a noble embarrassed by her ability to submit to a low-born teacher who resents everything about her. (978-1-63555-607-0)

Last Resort by Angie Williams. Katie and Rhys are about to find out what happens when you meet the girl of your dreams but you aren't looking for a happily ever after. (978-1-63555-774-9)

Longing for You by Jenny Frame. When Debrek housekeeper Katie Brekman is attacked amid a burgeoning vampire-witch war, Alexis Villiers must go against everything her clan believes in to save her. (978-1-63555-658-2)

Money Creek by Anne Laughlin. Clare Lehane is a troubled lawyer from Chicago who tries to make her way in a rural town full of secrets and deceptions. (978-1-63555-795-4)

Passion's Sweet Surrender by Ronica Black. Cam and Blake are unable to deny their passion for each other, but surrendering to love is a whole different matter. (978-1-63555-703-9)

The Holiday Detour by Jane Kolven. It will take everything going wrong to make Dana and Charlie see how right they are for each other. (978-1-63555-720-6)

Too Hot to Ride by Andrews & Austin. World famous cutting horse champion and industry legend Jane Barrow is knockdown sexy in the way she moves, talks, and rides, and Rae Starr is determined not to get involved with this womanizing gambler. (978-1-63555-776-3)

A Love that Leads to Home by Ronica Black. For Carla Sims and Janice Carpenter, home isn't about location, it's where your heart is. (978-1-63555-675-9)

Blades of Bluegrass by D. Jackson Leigh. A US Army occupational therapist must rehab a bitter veteran who is a ticking political time bomb the military is desperate to disarm. (978-1-63555-637-7)

Guarding Hearts by Jaycie Morrison. As treachery and temptation threaten the women of the Women's Army Corps, who will risk it all for love? (978-1-63555-806-7)

Hopeless Romantic by Georgia Beers. Can a jaded wedding planner and an optimistic divorce attorney possibly find a future together? (978-1-63555-650-6)

Hopes and Dreams by PJ Trebelhorn. Movie theater manager Riley Warren is forced to face her high school crush and tormentor, wealthy socialite Victoria Thayer, at their twentieth reunion. (978-1-63555-670-4)

In the Cards by Kimberly Cooper Griffin. Daria and Phaedra are about to discover that love finds a way, especially when powers outside their control are at play. (978-1-63555-717-6)

Moon Fever by Ileandra Young. SPEAR agent Danika Karson must clear her werewolf friend of multiple false charges while teaching her vampire girlfriend to resist the blood mania brought on by a full moon. (978-1-63555-603-2)

Quake City by St John Karp. Can Andre find his best friend Amy before the night devolves into a nightmare of broken hearts, malevolent drag queens, and spontaneous human combustion? Or has it always happened this way, every night, at Aunty Bob's Quake City Club? (978-1-63555-723-7)

Serenity by Jesse J. Thoma. For Kit Marsden, there are many things in life she cannot change. Serenity is in the acceptance. (978-1-63555-713-8)

Sylver and Gold by Michelle Larkin. Working feverishly to find a killer before he strikes again, Boston Homicide Detective Reid Sylver and rookie cop London Gold are blindsided by their chemistry and developing attraction. (978-1-63555-611-7)

Trade Secrets by Kathleen Knowles. In Silicon Valley, love and business are a volatile mix for clinical lab scientist Tony Leung and venture capitalist Sheila Graham. (978-1-63555-642-1)

Death Overdue by David S. Pederson. Did Heath turn to murder in an alcohol induced haze to solve the problem of his blackmailer, or was it someone else who brought about a death overdue? (978-1-63555-711-4)

Entangled by Melissa Brayden. Becca Crawford is the perfect person to head up the Jade Hotel, if only the captivating owner of the local vineyard would get on board with her plan and stop badmouthing the hotel to everyone in town. (978-1-63555-709-1)

First Do No Harm by Emily Smith. Pierce and Cassidy are about to discover that when it comes to love, sometimes you have to risk it all to have it all. (978-1-63555-699-5)

Kiss Me Every Day by Dena Blake. For Wynn Evans, wishing for a do-over with Carly Jamison was a long shot, actually getting one was a game changer. (978-1-63555-551-6)

Olivia by Genevieve McCluer. In this lesbian Shakespeare adaptation with vampires, Olivia is a centuries old vampire who must fight a strange figure from her past if she wants a chance at happiness. (978-1-63555-701-5)

One Woman's Treasure by Jean Copeland. Daphne's search for discarded antiques and treasures leads to an embarrassing misunderstanding, and ultimately, the opportunity for the romance of a lifetime with Nina. (978-1-63555-652-0)

Silver Ravens by Jane Fletcher. Lori has lost her girlfriend, her home, and her job. Things don't improve when she's kidnapped and taken to fairyland. (978-1-63555-631-5)

Still Not Over You by Jenny Frame, Carsen Taite, Ali Vali. Old flames die hard in these tales of a second chance at love with the ex you're still not over. Stories by award winning authors Jenny Frame, Carsen Taite, and Ali Vali. (978-1-63555-516-5)

Storm Lines by Jessica L. Webb. Devon is a psychologist who likes rules. Marley is a cop who doesn't. They don't always agree, but both fight to protect a girl immersed in a street drug ring. (978-1-63555-626-1)

The Politics of Love by Jen Jensen. Is it possible to love across the political divide in a hostile world? Conservative Shelley Whitmore and liberal Rand Thomas are about to find out. (978-1-63555-693-3)